SLEEP
TWO,
THREE,
FOUR!

SLEEP
TWO,
THREE,
FOUR!

A political thriller by John Neufeld

Harper & Row, Publishers
New York, Evanston, San Francisco, London

PN
N 482 ~

Library of Congress Catalog Card Number: 72-148422
Standard Book Number 06–024378–3 (Trade)
Standard Book Number 06–024379–1 (Harpercrest)

FIRST EDITION

12,935
11-74
3.79

SLEEP
TWO,
THREE,
FOUR!

1

"Don't!" the woman screamed, lunging at Chanler's cocked right arm as he took aim near the fireplace.

Without thinking, Chanler lashed out twice. His left arm caught the woman's jaw as she came near and sent her crashing into the corner behind him. He released his right arm at almost the same time, sweeping the mantle of his victim's remembered happinesses.

The rain of broken glass and heavy, sharp corners followed its owner, cutting her forehead and arms, bruising her left cheekbone. She stared breathlessly up at the Unit Leader, stunned.

Chanler did not look down at the woman. He hummed softly to himself as he moved away into another part of the small house, eager to join the other members of his Unit and then to call them off. Their work was nearly finished.

The woman stirred, modestly brushing her gray hair back into place as best she could. She heard the men upstairs. She heard her full-length mirror kicked in, the frame on her bed snapped like matchwood, the sheets and curtains torn as though made of newspaper.

A man in her kitchen methodically cleared each shelf. Glasses and china hit the shining, hardwood floor, rhythmically, endlessly. Dazed still, the woman smiled to think she had so much worth destroying. Idly, she wondered which man it was breaking things in there. Perhaps it was the young one, the one who actually looked kind. He seemed so young, so unlike the others.

Huddled in the corner, the woman knew it was no good fighting, no good worrying. This would have to be waited out. After all, it was just as she had been told. Out of nowhere. With no warning. And never—she listened carefully now—never any windows broken. No one on the outside could tell what was happening. What few sounds might have been disturbing to her neighbors were covered by the torrential rain and distant thunder of a late afternoon storm.

It was just as the President had said. Just as he had foreseen. How could a person feel safe, never knowing when or whether these gangsters might strike? How could a person defend what was hers, or count on other people to help, when no one knew whose home—perhaps his own—might be next? Was there ever reason or rhyme to the attacks?

The President said there was hope. Now that the C.I.A. and the F.B.I. had continuity, they also had purpose and confidence. The President had decided to stay in office another term. The criminals were warned, he had said. They could not hope to run rampant much longer. Not with the nation and its people so firmly behind him and his administration.

The woman sighed, neither believing her echoes nor wanting to disbelieve in them. The President was right, she thought. To have elections now would only divide the country. Would only make its people uneasy and mistrusting, empty of confidence.

Some of the men came downstairs. Their leader walked quickly to the front door. As he passed her, he deliberately kicked the woman's knee, although it seemed accidental.

2

She did not gasp. She lay there, waiting for it to be over, waiting for her daughter to come from work. She would never go to see the damage alone.

Chanler stood at the door, surveying his good afternoon's work. Then he frowned. That smart-ass kid, Berryman, what the hell was he doing?

Smart-ass Berryman was reaching down to the woman's side. Carefully he picked up a partially broken picture frame. Within it was the woman's only son, perhaps. In uniform. In the War. Briefly, Berryman wondered whether he was still alive or simply one more statistic in an endless battle. There was no way of knowing.

Berryman gingerly pushed what remained of the glass back into place, covering the image of the smiling, confident, maybe lost young man again for his mother.

The woman took the frame from Berryman as he offered it, silently. She had felt all along he wasn't cruel, like the others.

Berryman stood up. Chanler glowered at him. Deliberately, Berryman grinned in a way he knew drove Chanler up the wall. Then he stepped through the front door, past his leader.

Chanler followed, raging.

The woman, who was old enough to remember Germany and the beginning of a war forty-four years ago, lay there. Remembering.

2

D.J. Berryman ran through the rain to his car. He had parked several blocks away from the target house. He tried to think of the storm as cleansing him, washing away the sickness he always felt when a raid was finished.

Sitting in his car, trying to breathe normally, D.J. had a feeling that the sickness was growing. That he wasn't getting used to Chanler's brutality. That the raids weren't becoming automatic things. That soon, unless something happened, he would split down the middle, not knowing how to stop taking part in the violence, not knowing how to continue with a clear conscience.

D.J.'s attitude toward life had always been a simple one: don't think too much. Do what you did well and liked doing. Do what you had to as fast as you could so you could get back to doing what you like.

His activities with Unit Five embarrassed him, but he took comfort in knowing he never stole anything during a raid, and sometimes he thought he had saved one or two people extra injury and grief.

He was relieved a little when he felt sick, as he did just then. He knew he hated what he did. He knew he wouldn't ever make a life's work of it. How different he was from Chanler, who seemed to relish ugliness and pain.

Breathing more evenly at last, D.J. wondered if his father, too, reacted as Chanler did to the raids. For D.J. was no more appalled at the Unit's action than he was by his father.

4

Four years had passed since D.J. Berryman, Jr. had allowed himself to cry. He had been just twelve when he found out about his father and the woman. He discovered them accidentally. The Government had found out on purpose.

D.J. had frozen out his father then. It wouldn't have been such a difficult decision to make had he known then what he knew now: that his old man was the Regional Director of Wagenson's Special Forces Units.

There were twenty-four Special Units in D.J.'s town. According to President Wagenson's formula, that was all the population would support. Each Unit contained eight men. D.J. had once counted carefully: besides himself, President Wagenson and his Attorney General, at least 192 other people knew about his father. That meant D.J. Berryman, Sr. could be blackmailed a minimum of 195 times.

But D.J.'s father, a skillful and tastefully spectacular attorney in "real" life, had been a jump ahead of his son. Painting the raids as larks, he had talked D.J. into joining Unit Five, one that worked the east side of town where D.J. would know no one. There D.J. could—since he was already big for his age—terrorize and loot and raise general hell *as well as* help his father.

At first, D.J. had been curious, and vengeful. By learning about the Units and about his father, he thought he could sometime—not immediately, but sometime—get even with him. But within a few months, what had started as a plan for revenge had grown into a permanent attachment to the Unit. D.J. found himself betwixt and between. For while he had been allowed to learn of Wagenson's involvement in, and leadership of, the shock troops that terrorized neighborhoods and citizens, keeping them off-

5

balance and frightened and looking toward Washington for help and comfort, his father held the trump card: D.J.'s involvement in Unit Five. D.J.'s father could blackmail *him!*

And he probably would, D.J. thought. Without caring, he wondered whether his father would be told about the old woman and the picture frame. Chanler was supposed to report after every raid.

Shrugging, D.J. started his car. He didn't care about demerits and punishments. He felt certain the truce begun years ago with his father allowed him extra rope on a raid.

D.J. drove slowly, following traffic signals and warnings diligently and obediently. He liked driving. He got a lot of thinking done on the road. He was free, of everything, inside his own car.

D.J. was sorry September had arrived and, with it, school again. Summer always made him feel less guilty about Unit Five. During the year he had to manufacture one excuse after another to slip out of class early. So far the raids were broad-daylight ones. Nothing like coming home, D.J. thought, from a hot day at the office to find your kids scared out of a year's growth, your wife hysterical, your most precious possessions battered beyond fixing.

The rain seemed to be letting up. It had made the roads slippery and turnings precarious, so D.J. drove around the Ring Road cautiously, paying little attention to the checkpoints leading out of the city. Police cars parked squarely across the center of the road, poised for pursuit, manned by patrolmen standing guard at either end of the car. Checking permits to leave or enter took little time, either for driver or policeman. Unless, of course, an identity card was forged, a permit stamped red (no exit) or black

6

(no entry). Or a sticker not validated for that particular day.

But the barricades were simply part of D.J.'s day, as was his own special sticker for unlimited travel that he had gotten because of his work with the Unit.

The President had instituted restrictions on travel ten years ago, at the same time he introduced the homogenous communities that now circled each major city in the country. Travel restrictions needed no explanations. National safety and health spoke for themselves. Homogenous communities had not been much more difficult to explain. The idea, Wagenson had announced, was to minimize racial tensions. By separating blacks from whites, Indians from Chinese, handicapped from the healthy, fewer resentments could grow. Fewer people would be aware of the advantages or disadvantages of their neighbors. Little would be left to complain of.

D.J. had been a child when Wagenson made this scheme public. He hadn't been out of his own city since then. It hadn't occurred to him that others outside the city might live differently, or care more about living, than he did.

Recently, though, D.J. had begun to wonder about things. It was more than just a mounting sickness about the raids and his part in them. It was a growing uneasiness about almost everything he heard the President say. An impatience, a hot feeling in his gut that something wasn't being said or reported.

Turning off the road, nearing his own home, D.J. began thinking again about the rumors he'd heard since school started. About some kind of resistance group. About armed resistance to the President, to the Attorney General. Once, walking through a nearly deserted hallway at school, a tiny girl—she couldn't have been more than twelve, D.J. thought—appeared and offered him a proscribed document. She'd called it "The Bill of Rights." Nervously, and startled, D.J. had refused her gift. Now he had begun to wonder if he should have.

Maybe after school tomorrow, he thought, if there wasn't another raid, he would check in with Never Ready. Never Ready had a collection, small but real, of "secret" books. Most of them were sex books, D.J. knew. But maybe Never Ready had other things as well. Maybe Never Ready was part of the Underground.

There was so much D.J. hadn't really ever paid attention to. He felt now he should know more about what the country had been like before Wagenson appeared. He knew vaguely who Nixon was. He gathered the country had been pretty confused back then, what with Nixon always starting something new in the War and then blaming the other side for it. Still, D.J. considered, that was only at the beginning of the War's second decade. People weren't used to it yet. Their heads must have been spinning, though, he thought, never knowing who was telling the truth. Indeed, if anyone was. Wagenson, of course, had been around as long as D.J. could properly remember. He was used to thinking of him as having been President forever, although it was only his fourth term coming up.

Driving into his garage, D.J. decided he would definitely try to get to Never Ready tomorrow. He felt strong enough to fend off what the President called the "poisonous influences" of Never Ready's books.

3

Tank Wheeler walked through the parking lot toward the athletic fields beyond. She did not smile. Tank rarely smiled when anyone might see her. It wasn't that she was depressed, or serious, or even thinking about something special. Tank Wheeler just didn't smile. Except in her dreams.

Tank felt she was too big a girl to smile. To laugh or joke or kid around would only make people think she was the standard happy-go-lucky type. One hundred and thirty pounds and thirteen years were both, Tank felt, obstacles that could be overcome. In her dreams, Tank smiled because she saw another, different Tank Wheeler who was called by her given name, Julie, and who was lovely and slim. Tank was absolutely, positively certain that as she grew older she would grow beautiful.

Some people already could sense the beauty in her future, she knew. Her father, for one, every Sunday morning gave her a "man's point of view," he said, about how best to show off what she did have even now. And Never Ready Newman never stopped watching her in math class. He could hardly take his eyes off her. Tank knew it wasn't just because she was three years ahead of herself in math and had all the answers.

Tank stepped over a puddle from the rain of the day before. She heard the roar of an engine being revved. She looked around. D.J. Berryman's car was tossing gravel as

9

it backed out of its parking place. Tank walked a bit more quickly, careful to get out of range of the dirt she felt sure would spin back at her as D.J. took off forward.

Why the rush? Tank asked herself. D.J. was always hurrying somewhere when school finished. *Maybe he has a job somewhere,* she decided.

The cries from the intramural track meet met her ears. Tank frowned. She hoped she'd been right about Fatso Green. Even though he was a little older than Freddy, his weight and ungainliness had to make him slower. It just had to.

Tank walked slowly among her classmates—girls mostly, standing by to cheer their brothers and boyfriends. There were a few upperclassmen watching, too, but Never Ready was not among them.

Freddy Wheeler, who was always smiling even when other people would have cried, smiled even more broadly when he saw his sister. He walked carefully toward her. "Hi," he said.

"Hi," Tank greeted him somberly. "When do you run?"

"Not 'til the next race," Freddy answered. "Right now it's a relay. I'm not fast enough for that."

"That makes no sense at all," Tank said. "Why else are you running the hundred-yard dash?"

"Because everybody has to," Freddy said, smiling still. He looked down at his right shoe and rotated his ankle as best he could. "Everyone has to race at least once."

"You'll do just fine," his sister encouraged. "Where's Green?"

Freddy jerked his head toward his left shoulder. "He looks worried."

Tank looked critically at Fatso. He was nearing the limit, easily a hundred twenty pounds and not yet ten. A

10

little more weight and he would be shifted to a health camp. Tank sympathized with him. His pale face was dotted with nervous freckles, and his sandy hair sprouted in disarray. He stood alone, breathing deeply, trying to look ready and strong and fast and eager to run. But knowing that the first race of the year could send him away.

The first race of the year could send Freddy away, too.

"One thing," Tank said as she turned to face her brother, "at least the ground is soft, from the rain."

"And slippery," Freddy reminded her. "The only thing that would really help me is a new you-know-what."

Tank did know what. She had thought of nothing else for days. She kept imagining life without Freddy. She even had composed in her mind several letters she would write to him if he were picked up and sent away.

A shot rang out. The relay began. Cheers sang around Tank and Freddy who stood watching, not caring about the outcome of this particular race. Now Freddy, too, began to breathe determinedly, his wiry little body heaving up and down as he had seen other, better athletes do.

"It gets harder, you know, Tank?" Freddy whispered, his smile fading only a little.

"But just think," Tank said, "if you get through this, you're free for another year."

"I still have to do *some*thing."

"I think Daddy has the answer," Tank said. "Tennis."

"Except that it means I'm standing up all the time."

"At least it's better than football," Tank said, punching Freddy's shoulder softly to make certain he knew she was only joking.

A whistle blew. Time for the dash. "Go on, Freddy," Tank said. "It'll be O.K."

11

"Cross your fingers for me?"

"Always."

Tank's fingers *were* always crossed for Freddy. She agreed with her parents: she would never have been able to give him up, either. He was theirs, he belonged. Regardless. He was cheerful and quiet and fun to have around. His paleness never extended to his eyes which were eager blue, cornered by worry lines that were many years too old for him. His thinness and the painstaking way he put one foot in front of the other belied the sudden spurts of energy he could muster when he wanted, or had to.

But keeping Freddy had meant, so far, nine years of knotted fingers and whispered prayers and watchful living. It had meant that Tank's time was never her own unless Freddy was safe at home. It had meant that Tank had learned to smile and relax only in her dreams.

It meant one thing more. That Tank had learned to dream when she was very little. Dreaming was what she did now most easily, most happily, most of the time. One of her friends at school had once said that when Tank wasn't with Freddy, she was hardly anywhere at all. That crossing the street with Tank when she was dreamy and vague was the most dangerous, nerve-wracking experience in the world. You just knew you'd have to pick Tank up when she stumbled at the curb, since she hadn't even been aware of the street or its crossing or the danger in looking at the animals in the sky when an eight-wheeled truck was coming at her doing forty.

A dozen boys—six each from the fourth and fifth grades—stood in no special order at the starting line. The starter was telling them what to expect, how the countdown would sound. Tank turned away. She had never

12

been able to watch Freddy start a race. She had made certain that he knew her turned back meant only worry, and hope, not disinterest. Tank couldn't stand to see her brother fall, even if he only did so infrequently. Now, in a race, when so much was at stake—few knew how much— to watch the start calmly would be unbearable and a lie.

Tank stared at the big red brick building, sprawling wing after wing behind her. As she had done before, she concentrated on the inscription that ran above the windows on the wall nearest the fields. "Protest is generally negative in content. It is against some person or thing. It does not offer constructive alternatives and it is not conducive to creating the thoughtful atmosphere where positive answers may be formulated. Spiro T. Agnew."

No gun had sounded. Tank could feel the tension flooding her arms, then slipping into her fingers. Weakly she clenched her hands together across her body and read the words again. *Who was Spiro T. Agnew?* she made herself ask. Her own history class was already up to 1914. As far as she could recall, no one of any importance named Agnew had even been mentioned yet. He must have come later.

Still the race had not started. Tank's teeth began to grind together, something she had done for as long as anyone could remember. Left with only grass and trees to look at, a few remaining cars in the lot, and the empty windows set in red, she read the inscription for the third time.

What it was that disturbed her she couldn't have said. The three sentences reminded her of watching a youth rally last spring that ended in a pattern of teen-agers carefully spaced across a football field to spell the President's name. Tank hadn't thought much about it then, but now

13

she did. Since Wagenson had been President for as long as she could remember, why should he need any kind of cheer or pat on the back? Why would he care?

What she had been waiting for finally cracked behind her. Tank counted to five, slowly, and turned around. As she did, she heard the cheering begin to turn into jeering. She pushed her way through the spectators at the edge of the field, looking worriedly at the backs of the racing boys.

Laughter and shouting were added to the sounds around her as she caught sight of two boys trailing the rest of the field. Fatso and Freddy. They were running almost in tandem, their arms pumping back and forth in front of them as though that would help pull them ahead of each other. Tank watched as they duelled for several yards before she could stand it no longer. "Freddy!" she screamed. "Run!"

From the sidelines, suddenly, a figure stepped into the boys' paths, backwards as though he had been pushed. The red-headed boy fell back several steps before he was able to stop, correct his direction, and get out of the way again.

But the intrusion had had its effect. Tank began to smile as Robin melted into the crowd again, for Fatso Green had been put off stride. Huffing and puffing along as best he could, Fatso had outraced himself, and the break in his pace had thrown him completely off balance. Now he was racing out of control, unable to control his legs or even his direction any longer. He looked like a top fresh off its string, shooting across the floor destined to crash into a wall or a chair, dizzily collapsing in the nearest corner.

Falling forward in a straight line that should have pushed Freddy down too, had he been a fraction of a sec-

14

ond slower, Fatso went down. He sprawled flat, arms and legs spread-eagled, face down in the wet grass. Freddy crossed the finish line. Close to last. But not. Tank sighed.

She started forward quickly, looking for Robin Frye as she went. He seemed to have disappeared among the spectators. Tank wanted to thank him.

Freddy had stopped running a few yards beyond the finish, and was sitting on the grass, looking around and smiling. Even at fifty yards Tank could feel and see that his smile was a different one from what he normally wore. It was tense, and pained, and anxious to be gone.

Looking back briefly at the people standing around Fatso and laughing, Tank sank down to the grass beside her brother. "You were wonderful," she said to him, touching his shoulder.

"Robin was," Freddy answered in a whisper. "Without him . . ."

Tank looked at Freddy's foot. "How is it?" she asked.

"I think it's bleeding, but I'm not sure," Freddy said.

"Well," Tank said, standing up and pulling Freddy to his feet, "we'll just have to wait until we get home. Can you walk?"

On his feet, shaking, Freddy nodded. He looked around for Robin but could not see him in the crowd. People passed and glanced and talked and paid no attention to him and Tank. He looked at her and grinned. "Now," he said.

Together brother and sister walked slowly away from the playing fields. Freddy kept his smile firmly placed, his eyes straight ahead. Tank kept her arm around Freddy's shoulders, wondering how, without Robin, Freddy would have been able to stay at home yet another year without being discovered.

15

4

D.J. walked straight into his father's office. Miss Weinstein, accustomed to D.J.'s sudden entrances and exits, hardly took four seconds from her typing to look up.

"O.K.," D.J. said, sinking into a chair opposite his father. "What's so bloody urgent?"

D.J.'s father leaned back in his chair and smiled unpleasantly at his son. "What I like best about being a father," he said, enunciating very clearly, "is the friendly give-and-take, the mutual respect between child and parent."

"How nice for you," D.J. said, twisting around in his chair. "I hardly think you can imagine yourself, or me, as the typical father or child."

D.J.'s six feet one inch barely fitted the chair in which he sat. He had his father's dark, straight hair and very fine features. With one difference. When D.J. looked at someone, he looked straight and steadily. When his father did so, it was with a moving, fast, nervous kind of glance, as though searching distant underbrush for targets in the dark.

"All right," Mr. Berryman said. "Let's forget the wit. There's been a change of assignment."

"Whose?" D.J. asked. "Yours or mine?"

"Yours, I'm happy to say," answered his father. "I'm shifting you to Unit Nine."

D.J. whirled around toward his father. "Unit Nine!" he shouted. "Christ, that's our neighborhood!"

16

"I know," said his father.

D.J. looked at the well-dressed man sitting across from him. "No," he said evenly, after a minute. "No. Not on your life."

"This really isn't open to discussion, D.J.," said his father, just as calmly. "I need you in Unit Nine. The third man in a month has disappeared."

"Then why don't you concentrate on finding him?" D.J. asked. "Maybe he just got sick of the whole filthy business."

His father lit a cigarette and inhaled leisurely. D.J. waited. "Don't tell me what I should or shouldn't do, D.J.," said Mr. Berryman. "I wasn't picked for this spot for nothing, you know."

"Oh boy, I know," D.J. said. "Believe me, I know better than anyone. Except for maybe my mother."

Mr. Berryman's face darkened. He controlled himself with effort. "I've never promised, I've never threatened unless I meant it, D.J." he said. "As of this afternoon, you belong to Unit Nine. I couldn't care less whether it operates where your particular friends live. You're needed there. And you'll be there. Unless," and here he paused, trying to make D.J. understand the gravity of the pause and the thought behind it, "unless, of course, you'd prefer to have *all* your friends know about Unit Five and what you've been doing in it in your spare time."

D.J.'s eyes swung instantly back to his father's. His face grew pale and his mouth became a bitter, thin line. *No,* he thought, *no. I'm not ready for that, yet. I like being the regular me. I like being liked as the regular me.*

"Chanler's being switched to Nine also, to keep an eye on you. He'll be the new Unit Leader."

"Naturally," D.J. said sardonically. "Terrific."

17

"You're to meet him at 49th and Country Club at eight, tonight," D.J.'s father went on.

"For God's sake!" D.J. shouted, jumping to his feet. "We had a raid yesterday. Don't I even get a little time off?"

"Not when men are disappearing all around us," Mr. Berryman said, standing too. "There's something strange going on. We can't afford to let up, not for an instant. Not now."

D.J. nodded knowingly. "R. Thomas Wagenson's Number One Rule," he said. " 'If the People are Frightened, They will Respond.' Terrific."

He turned and walked as fast as he could from his father's office, wanting to put as much distance between himself and his father as possible, wishing he could do so permanently. He strode past Miss Weinstein without speaking, and ran for the elevator.

On the way down, he had a sudden, partly frightening and partly exhilarating thought. If there really were an Underground, if resistance was finally being organized and going into action, what would happen if he, D.J. Berryman, Jr., were discovered to be one of "them," one of the enemy?

5

The blue of his bathrobe and pajamas matched the deep blue of the marble tile around him. Robin Frye picked up his glasses from a shelf near the sink and looked at himself in the mirror. He still sometimes wished he had straight instead of curly hair, but now he decided he really rather liked the red.

Then, as the thought came again to him, he grinned at his reflection. He was nearly certain of it now. Soon he would be someone "who knew too much." He loved the sound of the phrase. He loved the danger in it, the secrecy.

Robin switched out the light and walked back down the hall, descending three steps to the landing and the door to his own room. He walked in and closed the door quietly behind him. As he had done for two years, every night, ever since Victoire had been taken away, Robin sat at his desk and wrote his report for the day. No one read these reports but himself. They were his alone, full of guesses and suspicions, full of hope and anger, full of dreams.

He picked up his pen and looked idly out the window, down onto the curving drive and to the ancient oak that stood darkly half way to the street. He saw his mother's garden with its neat, short winding paths, a garden that had grown more important daily since Victoire had gone, a garden whose flowers seemed to have grown up and around his mother's bending form each afternoon when he came home from school.

19

He looked upwards, scanning the top of the hill on the other side of the garden beyond which the Chase house stood, though he couldn't see it. All was quiet. There were few traffic sounds strong enough to carry up the long drive. He loved the way the house looked from the bottom of the gravelled entrance . . . tall and dark and turreted in brick and tile, like pictures of ancient Norman castles he had seen in school.

Conscious that he was staring out the window now without seeing, Robin shook his head sleepily and looked down at his notebook. He reread what he had been writing.

> *The officials were furious at me, threatening to turn me over to the Disciplinary Committee. But I was right. I knew they'd never take the time to run the race over again, and that it would take almost as much time to find a Committee Sergeant as it would to rerun the race. The funny thing is—*

Robin tried to remember what it was he had been about to write. With an assuring nod he leaned forward and concluded his thought.

> *The funny thing is that I know if I had to, I'd do the same thing over again. That, or maybe something even cleverer. Anything to keep Freddy from being beaten by Fatso and being deported. Maybe I'm brave without knowing it. Wouldn't that be something? Dangerous and brave!*

20

He looked at his words a moment and then closed the book, wondering both about his bravery and about his friendship with Freddy Wheeler who was, after all, three years younger than he was. Robin guessed it was made of admiration and worry, in equal parts.

Robin pushed his swivel chair around, letting it stop slowly so that he was facing his own doorway and the picture on its left, nearly above his bed. His sister Victoire, then only six, smiled down at him . . . a round little blond with orange ribbons in her hair and a mischievous but well-meaning gleam in her eyes. Robin stared.

He wondered if he'd ever see Victoire again. Whether a child who tested out as precriminal ever really recovered enough to be set free.

He tried to remember the tests he had taken when he was six and a half, or seven. Whatever answers he had given were the acceptable ones, the ones the psychologists wanted. He had a sudden thought: maybe they really wanted different answers. Maybe sometimes they didn't even care what the answers were. Maybe someone told them: "We need a few more children at Camp Forty-Six; a few more prehomicides would probably be best."

So in walks Victoire, unsuspecting and bright. Whatever answers she gives, truthful or not, loaded with extra meanings or empty of them, her answers don't really matter at all. They need her. At Camp Forty-Six.

Robin blinked. "They." He guessed that would mean Wagenson or someone in the Cabinet. But how could Wagenson know everything about every camp, or every town? Obviously, thought Robin Frye, he had informers planted, spies. *I am very small,* he thought, *but if I ever find one. . . .*

He *was* small and if he ever found a man or woman or

schoolmate he thought was informing, what *would* he do?

He stood up and opened the door to his room. He liked to spend his last few minutes each night with his parents if they were home. Since Victoire had been taken away, they seemed older, and sad.

He walked barefoot down the green-carpeted stairway and turned left, crossing the parquet hall to stand looking down into the dining room. His mother sat there, having a final cup of coffee, alone. In the kitchen behind her, Robin could hear Hestina and Mike clearing and washing. For some reason, at that moment he couldn't remember whether they had come from Czechoslovakia or Yugoslavia. It didn't matter, and he shrugged. "Good night," he said to his mother.

She started out of a dream and looked at Robin. She smiled. "Good night, dear," she said evenly. "Is all your work finished?"

"Yes," Robin answered. He waited, hoping his mother might say something more, something easy and maybe even a little funny. He knew she wouldn't.

He turned back across the hallway and walked past the living room toward the library, where his father would be. His right foot hit the carpeting as the front door behind him burst open with such force that the heavy oak slab squashed the doorstop against the wall and tore the plaster.

Startled, frightened, and then excited, Robin's first thought was *I don't believe it!* He stopped disbelieving as a huge man stepped into the hall, making directive signals with his arms at the men behind him.

"Kenneth!" Robin heard his mother shout from the dining room.

His father appeared in the doorway of the library. He

22

didn't move. No one seemed to move for a very long time. Then the man who seemed to be the group's leader took three or four determined steps in, giving his other men courage and the chance to move past him. "Man-o-man!" he said with a broad smile. "Is this gonna be fun!"

Robin counted six men, besides the leader. He sensed another man who seemed to be hesitating behind the others, but he couldn't be seen. All Robin saw was the leader himself, huge and strong and dark. Robin looked up into his father's face. He couldn't tell what his father was thinking; he made no move, nor even seemed to be breathing. *Do something!* Robin silently implored his father. *Do something!*

The leader waited, sizing up Mr. Frye. Mr. Frye stared back. Then, smirking because he knew he could wait for the older man's move, the intruder calmly walked into the living room. Humming a little, he turned on the lights and began his work. First, a lamp was thrown off a table and onto the hearth, shattering with shards of colored glass making the air seem laced with green and gold sparkle. Then the ripping of the full-length curtains began, as the first destructive noises came from upstairs and from the kitchen.

"Kenneth!" Robin's mother called again, screaming now. "Kenneth!"

Suddenly, Robin's father seemed to awake. As Mrs. Frye escaped from the dining room into the hall, Kenneth Frye moved through the door into the green-carpeted arena. The leader's hands now held a poker. Standing near the fireplace, he used it to dislodge and break and slash what he could reach.

Robin followed a pace behind his father, now truly frightened, and with an emptiness in his stomach. Every-

23

thing seemed suddenly speeded up; everything came at Robin at once. The sounds and cries and a thud from the distant kitchen. The sound of breaking glass and furniture above his head. His father lunging at the gang leader, dodging the poker as it sliced the air above his head, tackling the leader, throwing him against the brick wall of the fireplace and knocking him momentarily senseless.

Mr. Frye got to his feet quickly, turned the other way and ran toward the dining room steps. As he jumped down the three stairs, he was met by another man, younger than the leader, but even bigger. They struggled, the blows hardly audible, and then Robin saw his father fall back, clutching his stomach.

Without thinking how or why, Robin dove for the poker that lay beside the reviving Unit Leader. With it in his right hand, he swirled around to chase his father's adversary. Suddenly, the carpet came up at him and his glasses flew from his nose. Dazed, he realized that the man he had only sensed before did truly exist.

But before Robin could reach his glasses, the seventh man was gone, seeming to change places with the man who had battered his father. This man rushed into the living room, past Robin without touching him, and knelt to see to his leader, who rose, furious, as another scream and a second thud came from the kitchen.

Wild-eyed and breathless, the leader cast his eyes around the room. The same picture of Victoire that hung in Robin's room hung here, in oil. The leader smirked and moved painfully forward. He pulled a knife from his jacket and raised it to the canvas.

"Don't!" Mrs. Frye screamed, rushing out of a corner

24

with her hands held apart to grab the man's neck. He wheeled and blanched, suddenly afraid.

Glasses on, Robin could see now. He could see it happening, and he could see it was going to happen and there was nothing he could do. His mother flew past him, a blur of color and fury. The man had brought his armed hand down instinctively to hold his blade toward his adversary. Mrs. Frye, blinded by tears and shock, collided with him.

Not waiting to see what he knew he would see, Robin was up and rushing at the man, poker held straight out before him. Mr. Frye, recovered, flew to his wife as she fell, silently, to the carpet. Then suddenly a knot was formed. Blows and cries and curses rained in a dark circle. Robin hit out at anyone who wasn't his father; his father struck fast and powerfully, beating the Unit Leader's face bloody with two swift jabs, and then letting his hands fall to the leader's belly. Two men arrived in seconds to pull people apart, and Robin was lifted in the air from behind and hurled onto a couch along a wall some feet away. He saw his father felled from behind, still conscious, remembering to shield his wife who lay near by.

Robin then, finally, began to cry.

"Let's get out of here," the gang leader mumbled through bloody gums.

One of the two men bent down to help him to his feet. Two men who had been upstairs stood sheepishly in the hall, waiting. Behind them came two more men and low moaning from the Opiawas in the kitchen. Occasional crashes of unbalanced glassware finally reaching out for the kitchen floor were heard.

Robin continued to cry. He cried with his eyes closed.

25

He didn't want to see. He knew he would have to, but he didn't want to. At first he cried loudly, thinking in the back of his mind that maybe the Chases over the hill would hear and come to help. Then he cried quietly as he sensed movement around him, as he sensed a man being helped from the room, and as he heard footsteps in the hall leading toward the front door.

Suddenly Robin shuddered. A hand was on his shoulder. He opened his eyes and looked up, swallowing a sob. It was the seventh man. Robin stared.

"This wasn't supposed to happen," the man said. "This is never supposed to happen. I'm sorry."

Robin couldn't stop staring. "You!" he gasped.

The face above his froze. Then a hand gently reached out to take Robin's glasses off his nose.

In the hall, before leaving, D.J. ground the glasses into the hard, still-shining parquet.

6

Wow! Over and over again, Never Ready Newman breathed the word. He breathed it listening to a serene and strangely beautiful person named Baez; it slipped out hearing Country Joe and the Fish—*really weird looking,* Never Ready thought, watching the set. He pulled Wagenson's "degenerate" label from his memory and tried it on what he saw.

He gasped again as on his tiny screen three hundred thousand people began clapping their hands and singing *against* the War!

Never Ready felt elated in an odd way. He hadn't been prepared for any of this. Not for the color or the people or the music—strange-sounding chords and rhythms that, although he couldn't remember hearing them before, seemed somehow mysteriously familiar, as though when he was a child he might have danced and whirled to it in a circle as his parents laughed and clapped their hands for him.

He went to movies. He even liked going, in spite of the fact that he knew what he was seeing had been purposely filmed and shown to make him feel happy about his way of life, proud of his country, content to be who he was and where he was. He watched the Government networks and their shows. He hummed the approved tunes of the day.

But this was all something else, something Never Ready

27

could never even have dreamed about. And he dreamed a good deal. Mostly about sex. Mostly about what it would be like when it would be. About what it would be with Tank Wheeler. When he and she—but abruptly Never Ready stopped musing. He remembered where he was and with whom and what he was supposed to be doing. Out of the corner of his eye he looked at Gar.

Hunched over, staring intently at the television screen as though looking for one special face among the sea of faces flashing by, Gar Bennett tensed, the muscles of his back and sides straining against his shirt. His pale eyes seemed to x-ray each frame of the cassette, seeking support for some secret venture. His body was knotted in concentration. His hands were clasped beneath his chin, his huge forearms and biceps flexing and relaxing as remembered frames slipped by.

I never would have guessed, Never Ready thought, as he turned back to the forbidden film. He hadn't known Gar very long. Out of nowhere, it seemed, one day Gar had attached himself to Never Ready. Never Ready supposed it was because Gar was shy and he wasn't. Gar wasn't easy about making friends. Never Ready had hundreds. Gar didn't talk much. Sometimes Never Ready couldn't be stopped.

Still, who could have guessed that someone like Gar, that a Mister Teen-Age America type, would be mixed up in something like this? Even though he had heard, had overheard little things about the Underground, Never Ready never really believed it existed.

"Now!" Gar whispered. "Watch this, Never Ready. Watch!"

"I am," Never Ready whispered in return. He brushed the curly black hair back from his forehead and leaned out toward the set, not knowing what to expect or why whatever was about to happen was so important.

Gar tightened. There it was, that was the beginning! His ears prickled. The feeling of something good that always ran down his spine when he saw this grew in him. His eyes watered.

Three hundred thousand people stood up. As one man. Cheering. Applauding. Shouting. Stamping.

Never Ready was astonished. He had never seen anything like it. This was real, it was genuine. It wasn't some dumb demonstration on a football field that had been practiced for days. All these people were thinking the same thing; they were all *feeling* the same!

As the people on the screen began to sit down again on the hillside, Gar Bennett leaned back in his chair. "You see," he said. "It could happen. It really could."

"Wow!" Never Ready said. "Just wow! I mean, where did you get this? I never saw anything like it. Aren't things like that against the law?"

"They weren't always," Gar answered. "This is my dad's. Elizabeth found it."

"What do you mean, 'found it,'?" Never Ready asked. "You said your dad was part of the movement."

Gar smiled. "He is," he said. "But he didn't want us, the family, to know anything about it. He thought it might be dangerous. He was sure surprised when Elizabeth told him *we* were in it, too."

Never Ready took a deep breath and stood up. For a few seconds he paced along one wall and then returned, uneasy. Excited. Frightened a little. "What do you want me to do?" he asked Gar.

"Nothing now," Gar said quietly. "Just be with us. Just be ready."

Never Ready stopped moving and looked down at his friend. *Still water runs deep,* slipped through his mind. "O.K.," he said firmly. "I am."

"Good. I can't tell you much, not right away," Gar said. "Elizabeth's the one in charge of our group. I'm just a sort of handyman." He shrugged. "I'm not half so smart as she is."

"But aren't there any plans, any timetables for fighting, or anything?" Never Ready wanted to know. "I mean, it's great to be organized and all, but don't we have to *do* something?"

"That's the hardest thing, my dad says," Gar replied. "The waiting. Being patient until the right moment comes along."

"But how much longer do we wait?" Never Ready asked. "That's what the cassette shows. If we've got people, we've got power. The longer we wait, the harder it is to get him. He's already been around as long as God."

Gar smiled. "Not yet," he said, and he made a circular motion with one hand, around his neck.

"Enough rope for hanging?" Never Ready guessed.

"Exactly. My dad says he'll get too fat, too easy. That's when things will start, heat up."

"But *what* will start, Gar?" Never Ready was impatient. Now that he knew, he wanted to act. It was one thing being a fat little kid never ready, let alone able, to perform the slightest deed. It was something else being grown up and ready and able to do something that really mattered like this.

"One thing," Gar said. "It's Elizabeth's idea. You could help us recruit. You know so many people. Everyone likes you. We've got a few people, one or two in each grade. But you could probably get us the whole school."

30

Never Ready was surprised, and pleased. Gar—or rather, Elizabeth—was right. He could deliver the school. With his happy Irish-looking face and ready smile, he knew both the kids above him and the little ones grades below. He liked people.

"Can you get me one of those?" Never Ready asked, pointing to the cassette that had popped out of the television set.

"Maybe," Gar said. "But we've got other things, too, you know. Things most kids wouldn't even remember existed."

"Like what?" Never Ready felt a tightening in his stomach. There was so much he didn't know!

"Well," Gar began, "you know the sex books you've got?"

Never Ready nodded, reddening. He had trusted Gar when he let him see his secret library.

"There are other, better books, and films and music, too, just like those. Books that tell what *really* happened."

"You mean things that are all forbidden, like my stuff? Proscribed things?"

"Exactly," Gar said, bending down to pull out his book bag. "I brought some of them with me. Elizabeth said—"

The headlights of a car swung across the shuttered window. Gar stopped talking. Never Ready spun around, already counting. As far as he knew, his whole family was at home. Gar had broken curfew, but he'd been at Never Ready's for almost three hours now. It couldn't be the police, not this late. Besides, the Neighborhood Security Force never drove into a driveway unless a house's lights were all out, or unless they saw something suspicious.

Never Ready went to the window and pulled the curtain back one finger's width. He looked down at the car, its lights being turned off as its motor died. He squinted, but he couldn't recognize the form stepping from the car. The curtain dropped back into place.

Gar and Never Ready stood motionlessly, looking at one another. The front doorbell rang. They could hear voices. Never Ready shrugged. His father's voice wasn't raised, or angry. The other voice didn't seem authoritative or demanding.

Footsteps on the stairs, coming up to Never Ready's room. They stopped outside. There was a knock.

"Yes?" Never Ready called.

"Never Ready," a voice said. "It's me. D.J."

"What's *he* doing out?" whispered Gar suspiciously. "How does he rate a permit?"

"Come on in," Never Ready said.

D.J. opened the door and entered, smiling apologetically. He stopped when he saw Gar. An immediate question formed, but D.J. fought asking it. That was exactly the kind of thinking he hated, that even made him a little sick when he thought of it.

"Hi," Never Ready said. "You know Gar."

D.J. nodded and stuck out his hand. "Sure," he said. "You're our sensational new halfback."

Gar took D.J.'s hand and shook it, trying to smile. Still uneasy, questioning. Then he stepped back a pace. "It's good you have wheels," he said to D.J., putting his hand on top of Never Ready's television set, beginning ever so slowly to pull the cassette up and out of its slot. "I have to run the shadows." He slipped the cassette into his back pocket.

D.J. smiled. "Listen," he said. "Forget it. I have. O.K.?"

"Right," Gar nodded.

"How's your sister?" D.J. said.

32

"She's fine, thanks," Gar answered. "Listen, Never Ready, I better beat it. Thanks for your help."

Never Ready started. He'd been concentrating on something, a feeling he had of two people in one room, each waiting for the other to make a mistake. "Right," he said. "Glad to help. See you tomorrow, Gar."

Gar stepped past Never Ready and behind D.J. He turned, and motioning at D.J., he frowned a warning at Never Ready.

Left alone with D.J., Never Ready discovered a new sensation: fear.

"I just thought I'd drop by," D.J. said as Gar closed the door and went downstairs. "I mean, I was driving around and I— I—Never Ready?"

"Yeah?" Never Ready answered, beginning to perspire.

"Listen," said D.J., sinking into a chair. Never Ready suddenly noticed D.J.'s hands were shaking. "Listen, I've been driving around for an hour. I mean, listen—you're my friend, aren't you? I mean, if I had to tell you something, something personal and maybe a little horrible— well, could I count on you?"

33

7

Never Ready doubted Tank would ever turn into the great beauty Elizabeth Bennett was. Her nose was a little too round. Her hair was darker and not so well brushed. Her figure wasn't so tightly organized. *But her tits are bigger!* he thought triumphantly.

Miss Cain was rattling on in her high whine, her forefinger stabbing at a girl in the third row, her whole body pointed in its thinness into a question mark. Never Ready looked up at his math teacher for a moment, and then looked away. Class was nearly over. The day nearly done. Now everything important would begin.

Never Ready's heart beat faster than he thought it should have. But he couldn't help it. He had learned so much in so very few days.

He tried concentrating on Tank who sat two rows in front of him and to the right. He compared her solid features with his memory of Elizabeth's more patrician ones. And then, in his mind, he compared Elizabeth's face to her brother's. *Funny,* Never Ready thought, *how different twins can be.*

And then: *funny, how much difference there is in sameness.* For Never Ready had always thought of D.J. Berryman as someone who liked pretty much what he, Never Ready, did. Who did pretty much the same kinds of things and laughed at the same kinds of jokes. Who was older, but someone close enough to what Never Ready thought

34

of himself to be in the same pattern.

And yet, wow! Never Ready had said that word to himself a thousand times in four days. D.J. had a whole secret life!

Never Ready felt sorry for D.J. He had felt that way when D.J. sat despondently in his room and told him about his last raid. About little Robin Frye's mother. About everything. Never Ready wondered if telling made D.J. feel better. He doubted it.

At first, Never Ready hadn't known what to do. Except listen. When D.J. drove home, Never Ready had been unable to sleep. Should he tell Gar? Should he report to Gar's father or maybe to Elizabeth? Should he tell D.J. about the movement? Should he have tried to recruit D.J. into it, right there?

Instead of doing anything immediately, Never Ready opened the bag Gar had left in his room. For two days Never Ready read things that were strange and disturbing and exciting and angering. Finally he was ready.

On the third day he had talked to Gar *and* Elizabeth. Then he had been allowed to listen as Elizabeth met D.J. Never Ready wasn't really certain what he thought of Elizabeth Bennett, except that she was beautiful in a tight, controlled way. He did admire her coolness. He had to. Instead of being angry or horrified (as Gar had been), Elizabeth had set forth a plan D.J. could follow if he wanted to. If he was really upset about Unit Nine, if he was really ready to junk it, if he was really ready to join the other side. D.J. had jumped at the chance.

Afterwards, Gar had said what he held back from saying while D.J. had been there. Gar didn't trust anything D.J. said. If D.J. had really been ready to quit, why hadn't he just done so? Why ask for help? Why come to Never

35

Ready? Gar suspected a trap. He thought D.J. was a plant, trying to find out where the Underground was and who ran it. Gar wanted to kidnap D.J., to put him out of the way, out of the action. To Gar, D.J. was a traitor, a criminal, the enemy, just one more of "them."

But Elizabeth had cooled Gar off. And today, after school, after another raid—for D.J. had given Elizabeth the high sign during lunch—D.J.'s big chance to go straight would arrive.

Never Ready's heart kept pounding. He couldn't stop it anymore than he could stop the minute hand on Miss Cain's classroom clock from jerkily jumping down one minute at a time, to six. Anymore than he could stop the clouds that blocked the sun outside, and the distant thunder that seemed to ring the school.

Darkest before the dawn, Never Ready thought. *Nothing ventured, nothing gained.*

The bell rang. Never Ready stood up. So did Tank and the rest of the class, moving quickly out of the room and into the crowded halls.

Tank stood alone, waiting patiently for Freddy to turn up so they could start their short walk home. Never Ready stopped a few paces from her. *Why doesn't she ever even smile at me?* he wondered. *Nothing ventured,* he said to himself again.

"Hello, Julie," Never Ready said.

Tank started and turned around. She began to smile, but stopped half way through, making a polite little nod with her head. "Hello," she said shyly.

Never Ready didn't know what to say next. That he liked her dress? That he watched her all the time? That he secretly had wonderful plans for her? "It's going to rain," he said at last.

36

Tank nodded again. "What's your *full* name?" she asked.

Never Ready blushed. He looked down at his shoes. "Always keep your shoes shined and your hair cut," his father often said. He would have to try to do better about the shoe bit.

"I mean," Tank said, after waiting a moment, "A.J. doesn't really say very much, does it?"

"It stands for Anthony John," Never Ready said very quietly. "The third," he added.

"The third!" Tank Wheeler said, smiling finally all the way. The smile made Never Ready feel a hollowness in his chest.

Then Tank's smile went past Never Ready. He turned around. Coming slowly down the hall was Tank's brother and that poor little kid, Robin Frye. Suddenly Never Ready doubted that Tank's smile had been for him at all.

"Sorry to be so long," Freddy said to his sister.

"That's O.K.," Tank said. "Ready now?"

"Yes," Freddy said. "Robin's coming partway home with us."

Tank turned back to Never Ready. She looked at him for what seemed to Never Ready the longest minute in the world. All the noise in the hall seemed to die. "Goodbye, Anthony," she said as she finally turned her eyes and her face away.

Never Ready wanted to do something nice. Something sudden that would tell Tank he was human and kind. He watched the three start to move toward the double doors leading outside. "Hey, kid!" he called.

All three stopped and turned. Never Ready walked quickly up to them and put his hand on Robin Frye's shoulder. "I'm sorry," Never Ready said. "About your mother, I mean. I hope she gets better."

37

Robin smiled and stuck his finger beneath the bridge of his glasses. "Thanks," he said. "We do, too."

Never Ready squeezed Robin's shoulder and then, without looking to see Tank's expression, walked past the trio and out the doors.

"He's nice, isn't he?" Freddy said to Tank as the threatening air hit their faces. Tank smiled a little and nodded.

They walked down a flight of steps and across the grass, cutting through the parking lot to a street that would lead them back to their homes. Freddy chattered excitedly about something that had happened in one of his classes, every now and then checking Robin for reassurance. Tank walked in her own world, smiling on the inside, barely hearing the two boys beside her for the echo of her own name, "Julie," that sang inside her.

Suddenly Robin Frye stopped dead. He went pale, grabbed Freddy's arm, and pointed with his chin. Freddy looked as he was directed. Tank stopped too, looked back, and then looked forward.

D.J. Berryman, Jr. was slowly getting into a car that wasn't his own.

"That's one of them!" Robin whispered, suddenly frightened and then just as quickly determined. He let go of Freddy's arm and ran across the gravel as the car door slammed. The car spun dirt getting away.

"What's that kid doing?" Chanler asked angrily.

D.J. turned around and looked through the back window. He began to sweat. "God," he said, "I don't know."

"He recognized you!" Chanler said, turning a dark face on D.J.

"He couldn't have," D.J. answered weakly.

"Then what the hell is he doing?" Chanler asked. "I'll bet he's got the license number."

38

D.J. relaxed as the car hit the pavement and left Robin Frye behind. "That's easy to fix," he said.

"Yeah, it is," Chanler said. "But I don't like it. I don't like it at all."

Instantly, everything fell into place in D.J.'s mind. He had been right, he knew it certainly now. Chanler would *have* to be the fourth man in a month to disappear. He was glad he hadn't hesitated when Elizabeth had talked to him.

D.J. smiled and leaned back in his seat, winking at Chanler. "What's to like?" he said. "He's just a dumb little kid. No one ever pays attention to dumb little kids."

Never Ready, watching from a distance, turned and began his own way home as Tank and Freddy caught up to Robin Frye. There was nothing for him to do for a while. Then he would walk to the Bennetts' house to pick them up. Soon they would all know whether D.J. had been serious about what he had promised.

The darkening sky and the nearer thunder brought Never Ready out of his confusion. So much had happened and now Julie Wheeler. *Julie Wheeler,* he said to himself. *Julie Wheeler.* He liked the sound of the name. *Julie and Tony Newman.*

Never Ready blushed. All this had made him forget the Air Alert. He slipped his mask out of his book bag and fitted it over his nose and chin.

He quickened his pace and crossed a street. He had more important things to think about right now than Tank Wheeler, he reminded himself.

At last, he thought. *At last it is beginning.*

8

Half-heartedly, Freddy watched the cassette on public speaking. He had already showered and put on his pajamas, even though it was not yet five o'clock. He liked the snugness and warmth he felt when clean and ready for bed.

At home Freddy always felt safe. He felt protected. He was at ease. His parents treated him no differently than they did Tank, but he liked to remind them he was younger sometimes. He liked being the baby in the family. Sometimes Tank said this drove her nuts.

While Tank was dreaming about being beautiful as she grew older, Freddy dreamt about being older. About surprising his family. About becoming something that would make a difference. Something that would make his difference a difference no more.

One thing, Freddy thought, *when I grow up, I won't have to try so hard.*

The cassette was nearly finished. Dutifully, Freddy tried repeating the phrases: "Magazines can be easily read. Magazines can be easily read." The instructor on the tape explained why this sentence was important. M's and b's and r's were particularly hard for nervous people to pronounce quickly and well. The more often one was able to use words that began with these consonants, the better in time one would be able to say them evenly and smoothly, without a pause before.

"Magazines can be easily read," Freddy repeated quietly. Naturally he spoke with no hesitation at all. In his room. "Magazines can be easily read."

He squinched around on his pile of cushions and stretched out his legs. His foot stared up at him, slightly awry, very clean. He looked closely down at it, turning it evenly. There was no sign of the broken vessel. The blood had caked, dried, fallen off from the race a few days ago. Again, Freddy felt glad he had confided in Robin Frye. Someone had to know. Tank couldn't be around all the time. And even if Robin wasn't in the same class, he was closer than Tank was when school was in session. *Besides,* and Freddy smiled at his thought, *I like him.*

Still, if he were to play tennis, Freddy wasn't certain how he would get around showering with the rest of his classmates after practice.

He and his father had carefully looked at the alternatives open to boys in athletics. If Freddy could stand easily and move only a few feet forward, back, to each side, he could play tennis without much fear. And as long as Freddy was as small as he was, he could be coxswain for his class's shell.

Freddy knew his lungs were good. "Stroke! Stroke!" he could yell confidently and without pausing. He was only sorry that crew was a spring sport. Fall and winter activities seemed much more dangerous to him.

"Freddy!" came a call. He couldn't tell whether it came from his mother's room or from Tank, downstairs, in the kitchen. He decided to wait a moment.

"Freddy!" the call came again. It was his mother.

Freddy got up off the floor and wrapped his robe more tightly around his waist. He walked gingerly across the hard wood floor and over the knitted rug, which could

41

slide out from under him at any moment. This had been his father's idea, to keep Freddy on his toes, as it were, all the time.

Freddy walked down the carpeted hall to his mother's room. He could smell onions, and squash, and hamburger. *Tank must be experimenting,* he thought. Ever since his mother had become ill, Tank had cooked breakfast and dinner for the family.

"Hi," Freddy said shyly as he stood in the doorway to his mother's bedroom. He always felt shy with her. At least, he had ever since she had been carried to her bed when she came back from the hospital. Freddy knew his mother was dying. He didn't know what to do about it.

"I just wanted to hear about school," his mother said very quietly, with effort. "I like to know what's happening to you."

Freddy smiled and moved another few paces into the room. His mother brushed her brown hair back from her face and patted the bed near her. She wanted him to sit on the bed. Freddy smiled again and walked forward. Carefully, so as not to disturb her, he slid onto the side of the bed.

"Oh," his mother said, remembering. Her face was flushed. "Could you get me a glass of water, dear? I'm terribly thirsty."

"Sure," Freddy said pleasantly, easing off the bed again and moving to the bathroom.

He filled a plastic cup with cold water, letting the water run a bit before he did so. He knew that thirst was only one symptom. That his mother would always now be tired. That she would move only with care, and needed help even to do that. That she was losing weight no matter how much she ate. That when she ate she vomited nearly everything she had swallowed. That sometime soon she would be carried down the stairs on a stretcher and be taken to the hospital again. That she would not return.

He and Tank had looked up leukemia in the encyclopedia once a few months ago. What they both remembered most was that no cure yet had been discovered. And that no reason was given for the disease.

His father, though, felt differently. Freddy remembered hearing him, late one night, after he had had perhaps too much to drink, telling some friends what *he* thought had brought his wife down.

"The damned Army," he had said. "Just to get twenty years' worth of plutonium. To put together a hundred thousand bombs, to just stack those goddamned things up somewhere and then crow about nuclear deterents."

Freddy had been puzzled. For just before his father had said this, the talk downstairs had been of a nuclear power plant that had been built about thirty miles up the river from their town. The plant had been providing energy and electric power for towns around for almost ten years. Freddy remembered being suddenly frightened. Not for his mother, or his father. But for himself, for Tank. Maybe there really was fallout or something. Maybe the stuff that floated down the river really was dangerous. Maybe everyone he knew would get leukemia and die. Maybe, even now, the water he carried to his mother had some "hot stuff" in it. He, Freddy Wheeler, might have leukemia running through his veins at this very minute.

"What's the matter, Freddy?" his mother asked him as she took the glass of water. "Don't you feel well?"

Freddy smiled again. "Does it hurt, Mom?" he asked.

"No, dear, not really," his mother said. "I'm beginning to get used to it, a little."

43

"Maybe if you ate more," Freddy offered. "I mean," and he hesitated, smiling now just a little, trying to decide if it could be talked about, should be talked about at all. "I mean, maybe if there was more of you, it wouldn't happen so fast."

His mother smiled back at him. "I wish that were so," she said gently, touching his hand. "Now, tell me about school."

"Freddy!" It was Tank.

She was screaming. "Freddy!"

His mother pulled herself up against her pillows. There were sounds below, coming up the stairwell.

"Fred—!" Tank shouted again, and then stopped, short.

"Go, Freddy!" his mother whispered. "Go somewhere! It's them!"

"But Mom—"

"Do as I say, Freddy! Hide! Tank will be all right. They don't hurt people. Hurry!"

Two sounds floated into the bedroom. Things being smashed and thrown about downstairs. And on the stairs, heavy treads. More than one person was jumping stairs, two at a time.

"Freddy," his mother whispered. "Under here! Quick! Just get under the bed!"

Freddy felt foolish. He bent down and crawled beneath the big double bed, his robe's sash loosening and trailing out a bit behind him. He squirreled up in as small a space as possible, and waited.

He saw four feet enter the room.

"No trouble here," he heard one man say, laughing. "I'll just duck next door."

One pair of feet disappeared through the door. The

44

other stood in one place for a moment. Then Freddy heard a voice say, "I'm sorry, ma'am. It's my job."

His mother said nothing. The man moved away and into the bathroom. He opened the medicine cabinet and swept the contents of the shelves onto the tile floor. Freddy could see pill cases and tubes and bottles bouncing before they broke. Then he heard the mirror itself being cracked. The man's feet stepped back, away from the flying glass, and then turned, moving again into the bedroom.

Freddy held his breath. He heard funny sounds coming from Tank's room, and then from his own. Instinctively he knew his television set had been destroyed, his collection of glass boats smashed on the floor near his bookcase. He didn't hear the curtains in his mother's room being torn down, or the closet being ransacked, because he was thinking almost out loud, "Please, just let it be over. Please, please, please, let it be over soon."

A pair of boots stood in the doorway to his mother's room. "Finished?" they asked.

The man who had apologized to his mother answered. "Finished. Nothing here."

"What's that?" asked the pair of boots.

"What?" answered the loafers.

"There," the boots pointed, "under the bed."

His mother said nothing. Freddy stopped breathing.

The boots moved to the bedside. *He won't get down to look,* Freddy thought. *He won't, I just know he won't.*

And he didn't, the man with the boots. Instead, he reached down and grabbed the belt that had come loose from Freddy's robe. Evenly, strongly, he pulled.

Freddy squirmed, trying to let the belt slip through the loops on his robe. But he was caught. He felt himself being drawn slowly, rubbingly, from under the bed. As

45

his head finally appeared and was free, he looked up into a surprised face.

"Well!" said the man with boots on. "What a brave little boy we have here!"

Freddy did not smile. He tried to speak, but he could get nothing clearly out. He was still being pulled out from under his mother's bed. His mother had not spoken.

"Chanler," said the man with loafers on, "he's just a little kid. Leave him alone."

"Shut up," Chanler replied angrily. "I'm not going to hurt him. I just want to get a good look at a kid who's such a great family defender."

"That's not fair—" Freddy started to say and then stopped. He didn't think he wanted to explain why it wasn't fair.

Chanler picked Freddy up roughly, heaving him to his feet by his shoulders. Freddy's feet were in the air for a fraction of a second too long. When Chanler set him down, Freddy fell on his side.

"Freddy!" his mother gasped.

"What the—" Chanler started to say. Then he saw. He bent down.

Chanler held Freddy's foot in his hand a moment. "I'm damned," he said. "I'm absolutely damned."

"Chanler," said the other man, "let's get out of here. This isn't any of our business."

"Shut up, I said," was Chanler's answer. He let go of Freddy's foot. "It's been years since I saw anything like this. Ever see one like it, Berryman?"

D.J. shook his head.

"Please," Freddy's mother said.

"Listen, lady," Chanler interrupted. "Either you're a brave and very smart lady, or you're a brave and very

46

dumb one." He turned and started toward the door and the stairway beyond. Just before he disappeared, he turned to Freddy and winked. "See you again, kid."

D.J. stood motionlessly a moment. Then he remembered what would happen later, on the way home. He felt very tall. "Listen, kid," he said as he bent down to talk to Freddy face to face. "Don't worry about this. I won't tell anyone. And he," D.J. moved his head towards the departed Chanler, "he won't be able to."

D.J. stood straight again and tousled Freddy's hair. Freddy tried to smile a thank you. It was suddenly very hard.

D.J. strode toward the door of the bedroom. Going through, he turned and gave Freddy a thumbs-up sign.

Freddy sighed, hearing the footsteps bouncing very fast down the stairway. Then he remembered something.

What about Tank?

9

Never Ready's stomach was knotted. It gurgled a little and then stopped. His breath stopped at the same time. A car was being driven slowly through the park toward him.

He looked quickly around an edge of the rock. Elizabeth was standing, waiting, with a smile on her face. Composed, calm. *In charge,* Never Ready thought with awe.

Gar was lying flat on the damp ground beside him, his hands free and his fingers moving ever so slightly back and across the grass. Gar saw the car, too. Never Ready tried to take comfort in Gar's strength. He didn't want to think what might happen if something went wrong.

"Is that her?" Chanler asked D.J., pointing up the hill.

D.J. looked up and nodded "Yes," he said, smiling. "I knew she'd wait. She's very loyal."

Chanler squinted into the dying sun as he drove closer to the girl, trying to get a better look.

Elizabeth stood very straight. She remembered she was supposed to be D.J.'s girl. She smiled. She wondered what it would be like if she really were that. She raised her hand and waved. The car came up the hill, nearer.

"From here," Chanler said, with a touch of envy in his voice, "she looks like some sensational piece."

D.J. said nothing. He didn't care what Chanler thought. He was only interested in what would happen when the car stopped.

Elizabeth smiled more broadly as Chanler idled his

48

motor a few feet away, down a slight rise from where she stood. Gar and Never Ready crouched ready for action behind the boulder on her right. D.J. started to get out of the car. "Hi," he called. "Come on down. I'd like you to meet someone."

D.J. watched as Elizabeth gingerly stepped over a few small rocks and came toward the fender of the car. Chanler rolled his window down and leaned his head out. Elizabeth stopped near the headlights.

"Hello," she said, nodding. "I'm Elizabeth Bennett." She wondered suddenly if she should have used another name.

"Well, hello," grinned Chanler. "Bruce Chanler. I'm a friend of D.J.'s."

"I've heard him mention you," Elizabeth said. As she said this she doubted she should have. D.J. was out of the car altogether now, and coming around behind the car toward her.

Elizabeth moved closer to Chanler, noting with relief that his door was unlocked.

Never Ready felt numb.

"Have you seen the view from here?" Elizabeth asked Chanler pleasantly, putting her hand on the door handle.

Gar sprang from his position, whirling around an edge of the boulder. Never Ready was a few feet behind him, having come around the other side. Elizabeth pulled the car door open as fast as she could.

But it wasn't fast enough, by a fraction of a second. As the door swung open, leaving Chanler exposed to the group, the edge of the door hit Gar who was running full tilt in a crouch to Elizabeth's side. There was a thud. Gar fell back onto the grass, stunned.

"Jesus God!" Never Ready muttered.

49

D.J. leapt the few feet from where he stood to reach into the car, grabbing Chanler's arm and starting to drag him out. Never Ready dropped the twine he held and reached past D.J. to get one of Chanler's legs, or at least his belt.

Realizing he couldn't hold his ground inside the car, Chanler took them both by surprise. He leapt out toward them, pushing both away with his free hand and spinning free of their grips. He took a step sideways and grasped Elizabeth's arm. Dragging her with him, Chanler began running up the hill. As he ran, Elizabeth tried to drag her feet, to squirm out of his grasp. Chanler was too strong.

Atop the knoll, Chanler stopped and spun around. He forced Elizabeth into a position between himself and the car below. He reached into a side pocket for his switchblade.

Never Ready and D.J. froze. So did Elizabeth.

No one spoke or moved. Gar groaned and tried to sit up.

Chanler smiled, relieved. "Pretty close, gang," he admitted. "Almost but not quite. No points for a miss."

D.J. saw everything at once. If Chanler escaped, they would all be picked up. Preventive detention. Assault on a Unit Member, though it would probably be called something else. "Chanler," he called, "wait!"

"I'll wait, buddy. I'll wait one minute, maybe even two, for you to get away from that car. Far away!" Chanler was commanding now. He felt better.

D.J. bent down to help Gar to his feet. Never Ready took Gar's other arm. "What do we do now?" Never Ready whispered urgently.

From Gar's bent head came an answer. "Pretend I'm

50

still out. You can't lift me. I've been really hurt," he said under his breath. "Tell Chanler he's got to take me to a hospital."

"But Gar—" D.J. said.

"Alone?" asked Never Ready.

"Do it!" Gar whispered. "Just do it!"

"Well," Chanler called down, his arm around Elizabeth's throat and his knife in readiness. "I'm waiting."

"Chanler," D.J. said loudly, "this guy's really hurt. You've got to get him to a hospital."

"Sure I will," Chanler laughed. "And then I'll put all of you in the beds right next to him!"

"Oh!" Never Ready said.

"We'll put him in the back seat, O.K.?" D.J. called out.

"O.K.," Chanler answered. "Then back away. And I mean—away!" He tightened his grip on Elizabeth and took a step forward as Never Ready and D.J. started again to lift Gar.

With Elizabeth held before him, Chanler began walking carefully down the rise. Elizabeth pushed against Chanler's pushing, evenly, without seeming to be angry or afraid. Chanler tightened his arm around her throat each time she was reluctant, and together, step by step, they moved toward the car.

Then, suddenly, Elizabeth shouted "Gar!" as she dug an elbow into Chanler's stomach and bent forward with well-practiced speed, throwing Chanler off her back and onto some rocks.

The three boys looked up. Gar jumped free of D.J. and Never Ready and started up the hill.

Chanler landed on his side, his left arm crunched beneath his body. He wasted no time moaning as the pain shot up into his shoulder. He rolled on his side and down a

51

few feet, managing to trip Gar as he ran. Gar fell and reached out for Chanler at the same moment.

Together the two rolled farther down the hill toward D.J. and Never Ready. Before either of them could jump to help him, Gar had managed to stop rolling and, miraculously, to land on top of Chanler, sitting on Chanler's chest and pinning his arms back with his knees.

Never Ready had never breathed such a sigh. "What do we do now?" he asked as he handed Gar the twine he had dropped earlier.

Elizabeth stood next to Gar, towering over Chanler's squirming form. "Take him home," she said coldly. "My father will want to talk to him. First."

Chanler stopped struggling. He looked up at Elizabeth. She was unscathed and triumphant. "Bitch!" he spat at her.

Elizabeth nodded and beamed down at him. "I know," she said. "Isn't it wonderful?"

10

Never Ready wished that he had been a Boy Scout after all. The knot looked tight enough. It was certainly big enough—doubled back and under many times—but it was still not a real knot, one with a name that was untieable. He stood up. It would have to do. Maybe he should have tied the rope around the chair legs, too, just in case. Still, Gar and D.J. were nearby, and Mr. Bennett had just come down the stairs.

"Mission accomplished, I see," Mr. Bennett said quietly. He ducked beneath some pipes and walked around a few storage boxes the family had put in the basement when they'd moved in several months ago.

Never Ready was surprised. He had pictured Gar's father as tall and dark and hugely strong, taciturn, too, with a deep, clipped voice. But what he saw was a pleasant-looking man, of only medium height, trim but not strong the way Gar was.

"I suppose we'll have to order more food now, won't we," Mr. Bennett continued, walking up close to Chanler. "Although this one's a little paunchy around the middle. Maybe a diet would do him some good."

Chanler didn't speak. He watched carefully. Never Ready thought he looked as though he were memorizing every word and every face so that later, when he—Never Ready stopped thinking. He went again behind Chanler's chair and looked at the knot. *A stitch in time,* he thought, in spite of himself.

53

"This is D.J. Berryman, Daddy," Elizabeth said. "He's the one we told you about."

Mr. Bennett stuck out his hand for D.J.'s. "I'm glad you're here. I'm grateful you did what you said you would."

"So am I," D.J. said seriously. "I just wish I could undo some of the other things I've done."

"You already have," Mr. Bennett said kindly. "You know," he continued, walking back and forth across the cement floor, "I've tried to think what else you could do for us, if you stayed in your Unit."

"But sir," began D.J., "I thought this—"

"I know, I know," Mr. Bennett said. "You want this to be the end. Well, I guess it is. We're stumped, all of us. The only thing you could do, I guess, would be to warn the targets of your attacks."

"I don't want to go on, sir," D.J. said. "Besides, I'm afraid I couldn't even do that—warn people, I mean. We're never told where we're going. Only the Unit Leader knows." D.J. pointed to Chanler. "It's only by accident sometimes you find out what their names are."

Elizabeth took a step forward and put her arm through her father's. "But now that another man has disappeared, D.J., isn't there a chance you could be made Unit Leader?"

"I don't think so," D.J. said. "I don't think my father trusts me that way."

"Where do we take him, Dad?" Gar asked, motioning at Chanler.

"I'll handle that a little later. Maybe tomorrow. I don't want you to know everything. It's safer this way." Mr. Bennett looked around the group. "Never Ready," he said, "you look a little pale. Are you all right?"

Never Ready started. He couldn't honestly say he felt

wonderful. It was too hot in the basement. Indian Summer was lingering a few minutes too long for Never Ready. "It's been a pretty scary day," he said. "I guess I'm still a little nervous."

"We almost didn't make it at all, sir," D.J. explained.

Mrs. Bennett came down the cellar stairs, interrupting D.J.'s recounting of the group's adventures in the park. She smiled at each young person and then walked to Chanler. She looked down at him. Never Ready was struck by the similarity of Mrs. Bennett's look to the look Elizabeth had given Chanler when Gar had captured him.

Mrs. Bennett turned and winked at her daughter. "He's a big one, isn't he? I wonder how he got started in this."

Chanler stared at the woman but said nothing.

Without warning, Mrs. Bennett whirled around and struck Chanler across the mouth with her open hand. The slap sang around the cellar walls.

"Nora," Mr. Bennett said softly.

"I just wonder," Mrs. Bennett answered, smiling again and walking a few steps away from Chanler, whose eyes were still watery, "how he missed testing out. I mean, obviously, this is one they could have used."

Never Ready listened as he had never before been conscious of listening. He felt he was getting smarter as he lived longer. Maybe Elizabeth and Gar had had a brother or sister taken away. Someone who had tested out badly.

"Besides," Mrs. Bennett almost laughed, "I hardly ever get a chance to see one of them in person."

Mr. Bennett touched his wife's shoulder. "We could use some food, Nora."

She nodded. "There's nothing more we can do anyway, right now. Not until it's dark."

Mr. Bennett motioned the four young people to follow his wife up the stairs. Never Ready gave a cautious look at Chanler.

"It'll be all right," Mr. Bennett reassured him. "There's only one way out of here, and that's past us upstairs. Don't worry."

Chanler grinned unpleasantly at Never Ready as the group climbed up the stairs.

Chanler allowed a few minutes to pass. He could hear talking and the clink of glasses, the clunk of silver being rested on plates above him. He waited a little longer. He breathed quietly, deeply. He pulled his legs closer to the legs of the chair, and tensed them.

Carefully holding his arms out free of the back of the chair behind him, Chanler cautiously rose to his feet. His tied hands cleared the top of the chair. He took a few quick steps to the bottom of the stairway and listened. He let his hands and arms relax. He had held them tense, straining as Never Ready tied them. Perhaps when the time came, he had thought, the extra room in the knots would make the difference.

It didn't. Swearing to himself, Chanler put a foot on the first step. It made no sound.

He climbed the stairs carefully, taking time to settle on each step before beginning to take the next. Soon he was at the top, peering out the doorway, looking into the kitchen and the dining room beyond.

The Bennetts and Never Ready sat facing him; Elizabeth, Gar, and D.J. sat with their backs to him. Chanler was grateful. That Bennett kid was strong, and probably fast, too. He didn't want to tangle with him again if he could help it.

He looked around the kitchen. The back door was

56

open; only the screen door stood between him and freedom. But with his hands tied behind him, Chanler wouldn't be able to open it quickly enough. There was only one way to go. He took another deep breath.

It was Never Ready who saw Chanler streak across the kitchen. He gasped as the Unit Leader threw himself against the screen and snapped its frame as he plunged through.

"Look!" Never Ready cried, tipping his chair over as he struggled to stand.

Mr. Bennett sprang from his chair and ran into the kitchen, just in time to see Chanler get to his feet and disappear through a hedge that separated his house from the one next door.

Never Ready, his face white but for two reddening spots above his nose, followed, and bumped clumsily into Mr. Bennett.

Mr. Bennett turned around. "Hold it!" he shouted.

Never Ready turned to see Gar and D.J. halt in their tracks, heading toward the front door. They turned.

"But Dad," Gar said, "if he gets away, we're all in trouble."

"Trouble's too small a word," added D.J.

"I know," Mr. Bennett said, walking back into the dining room. "But you won't find him now. You'd chase around trying to track him. But he can head in any direction, hide behind any bush."

"Curfew will get him first," said Mrs. Bennett, standing up.

"But he'll tell the Security Guards!" moaned Never Ready.

Mr. Bennett clenched his hands together, cracking his knuckles. "I just wish," he said after a moment, "we'd had time to finish eating. The food would have stood us in good stead."

"Arthur!" said Mrs. Bennett, a happy note in her voice. "Now, finally?"

"I'm afraid so," her husband said. "I wasn't sure this was the time, but I guess now is as good a time as any."

"What, Daddy?" Elizabeth wanted to know. "What are you talking about?"

"About whether we're ready yet," Mr. Bennett explained. "Whether the moment has come to really begin our fight, in the open."

"Underground," Mrs. Bennett said with a smile. "In the open, underground."

Never Ready's pulse jumped. Visions of tunnels and sewers and bloodhounds flooded his mind.

"The only thing is," Mr. Bennett said slowly, thinking as he spoke, "I'm afraid we're not ready to handle this many people all at once."

"Arthur!" Mrs. Bennett gasped. "We *have* to be ready. We're not going to leave any of these kids on their own. Not now."

"I don't know what we can do," her husband said. "It seems unfair. D.J. and Never Ready have risked just as much as Gar and Elizabeth have. But we can't take everyone. Without warning, and time to plan, we just can't."

D.J. understood. He wasn't surprised about going underground. He wasn't even particularly afraid of being out on his own. He looked at Never Ready, wondering how he felt.

"Don't worry about us," Never Ready said, surprising even himself. "We'll be O.K. I guess," he added softly.

"But where can you go?" Elizabeth asked. "You'll be hunted anywhere you stop."

58

"No," D.J. said, "we'll make it. I'll sneak back and get my car. It's got an exit sticker on it. If we can get started before Chanler reports to anyone, we'll have a fair enough chance."

"You'll never get away," Gar said. "Besides, Chanler will grab your father, too. He'll think he was in on it. He certainly won't stop at not getting us."

D.J. took a big breath and nodded to Gar he agreed. But what else could he hope for? He looked again at Never Ready and tried to smile encouragingly at him. Never Ready shrugged and made a face he hoped resembled a smile.

"Daddy," said Elizabeth after a moment, "we can't go with you, Gar and I."

"What?" Mr. Bennett said. "Don't be silly."

"We can't," Gar said. "We convinced D.J. that what we were doing was right and safe and would make a difference. It hasn't."

"We'll have to take the same chances D.J. and Never Ready do," Elizabeth added. "Maybe, if we can get that far, we can join a group in Brookhaven."

Never Ready felt better suddenly without knowing why. The danger hadn't lessened any. But the loneliness had.

"God!" Mrs. Bennett said. "To fight, to start at last!" She turned away and went into the kitchen, opening cupboards and selecting things with both hands.

Elizabeth smiled at her father. He tried to smile back, and then he did genuinely, with pride. He nodded. Elizabeth joined her mother in the kitchen.

"I'll have to phone my parents," Never Ready said. "They should know."

"We'll take care of that," Mr. Bennett said. "With wiretapping and surveillance, a message of some kind is probably safer than the phone right now. They won't be worried, so don't you be, Never Ready. You're a strong kid. They've done a good job with you."

Never Ready blushed. Then he smiled more to himself than at Mr. Bennett or Gar or D.J. *Don't cry over spilt milk* had come into his mind. Remembering things like that always calmed him down.

Gar looked at his father and then turned away. He felt angry, and he felt guilty about feeling angry. If it weren't for D.J. and Never Ready, he and Elizabeth could go with their parents. Gar felt cheated. Elizabeth was always smart, ahead of him in so many ways. And Gar had been protective but a little jealous of his baby brother. When Charlie had tested out and been put away, Gar had hoped he and his father could work together on something, could get to know one another better and come to like each other, as men. Now even that chance was gone. *One thing is for sure,* Gar thought. *I'm going to do something that counts. I'm going to lead.*

"I'd better get going," D.J. said. "There's no telling how fast Chanler can get himself together. If we want my car, we'd better move."

"D.J.!" Gar called as D.J. started to move away.

"What?"

"Stop and think a moment. Is there anyone else, anyone besides your father," Gar said, "that Chanler would go after?"

D.J. looked puzzled. "I don't know," he said. "What do you mean?"

Mr. Bennett nodded and looked approvingly at Gar. "People on your raids," he suggested.

D.J. waited, trying to remember. "Well, there was this one little kid. There was something wrong with his

60

foot. Like it was damaged or something and he should have been in a health camp."

"Did Chanler see him?" Gar asked.

"We both did, at the same time," D.J. said. "You're right, Gar. We'll have to get that little kid, too."

"Who was he?" Mr. Bennett asked. "How far away?"

"Pretty near here, I think," D.J. said. "His name was ... his name was Wheeler, I think."

Never Ready's heart sank. "Did he have a sister?" he asked. "Was there a girl there?"

D.J. thought a moment. "Yes," he said, "downstairs. Chanler clipped her as he went by."

Never Ready felt sick.

Elizabeth came back into the room, carrying a well-packed canvas bag. "We'll have to take them both," she said. "I mean, if the little boy is hurt in some way, his sister should be able to take care of him."

"He's not hurt so much," D.J. said. "Just sort of shaped funny."

"You go and get them," Gar commanded his sister.

"I'll come, too," Never Ready chimed in, a new feeling of protectiveness stealing into his heart.

"D.J.," Gar went on, "I'll go with you, just in case there's trouble. We'll all meet at those people's house— Wheeler's. You know where it is, Never Ready?"

Never Ready nodded that he did.

"O.K.," Elizabeth said. "You can carry this." She handed the canvas carryall to Never Ready.

Gar came closer to his sister. "Matches?" he asked. "Paper? Bandages? Water?"

Never Ready stared at Gar. Everything was changing so fast!

"Salt? Chocolate?" asked Mr. Bennett.

61

Elizabeth smiled. "It's just like yours, Daddy," she said. "Just the same."

"Let's get going," Gar said. "We don't know how much time we have."

Mrs. Bennett came into the room as Mr. Bennett held out his hand to stop Gar from leaving so fast. "Easy," he said gently. "You wouldn't mind saying good-bye to your mother and me, would you?"

Gar blushed and reached out for his father's hand.

Mr. Bennett smiled. "You know," he said, "this isn't the first time families have had to divide like this. Maybe it's the first time for us, here in our own country. But there's one thing we all have to remember." He paused and included each person in his gaze. "The kind of government we're going to fight has been fought before." Mr. Bennett's face broke into a wide smile. "And it's been beaten."

Mrs. Bennett went up to Never Ready and gave him a heartening embrace. She went next to D.J., and Gar, and finally to Elizabeth, doing the same thing. As she held Elizabeth, she whispered loudly enough for everyone to hear, "We're very proud of you, Elizabeth. We always have been."

Elizabeth said nothing. She looked over her mother's shoulder and smiled at Gar reassuringly.

"We'll keep tabs on you," Mr. Bennett said. "If you get to Brookhaven, there may even be a message."

No one moved. No one seemed to want to move, to begin. Finally Mr. Bennett nodded at his son, and then turned away, walking into the kitchen to look out the torn screen.

Mrs. Bennett smiled happily as each of the four young people passed her. Then, after the screen door had closed and when she could no longer see shadows moving among the bushes, she turned and walked quietly to her husband's side. "Arthur," she said, "it's time. We have to go now."

Mr. Bennett nodded. He took his jacket from his wife and put it on.

"Arthur?" Mrs. Bennett said. "I hope you'll be proud of me, too, now."

11

The Security Guard's car swung around a corner, pinning D.J. and Gar in its headlights. D.J. checked his watch. They were still under curfew.

The car drove slowly by, the window on the car's curbside rolled down so one of the two guards could get a good look at the two boys.

For some reason, D.J. turned to face the guard and gave him a saintly smile. And a wave. The guard nodded severely, and the car rolled on.

"That was dumb!" Gar said.

"I just felt like it," D.J. explained. "Why not?"

Gar said nothing. He decided to wait. If he wanted to lead truly, he didn't want to make D.J. dislike him any more than necessary.

The boys walked quickly on, turning once to the right, once to the left. They spoke little.

D.J. would have liked to see his mother once more. Before leaving. She had been away for such a long time that he had trouble remembering that his house was also hers. But he liked his mother. And now he realized that probably he missed her, too.

He didn't know what he felt toward his father. He wouldn't miss him, that was for sure. But perhaps D.J. should have warned him. Phoned from Bennett's house, maybe. After all, was it entirely his father's fault that he had been used, that he had been forced into being Regional Director?

Yes, D.J. answered himself. It was. He could have refused. He could have fought, the way the Bennetts did. He could have admitted everything. He could have been not afraid, not greedy, not ambitious.

But that, D.J. reminded himself, would have meant that his father just wasn't his father. That would have been a different man altogether.

It should mean something, thought D.J. despondently, that he *was* his father: D.J. Berryman, Sr. He looked to his side and watched Gar walking straight ahead, eyes on the alert. He wished, and he knew he wished as a child would, that he had been Mr. Bennett's son instead.

Gar, for his part, was glad Elizabeth was going to be along. Elizabeth had always been the quicker one. Gar just didn't think as easily or as positively as his sister did.

Not that he was going to give up leading. But he wondered if he had been right to compensate the way he had. All the time spent exercising, lifting weights, measuring muscles' growth, eating the right foods. It was great to be a halfback on the varsity when you were only a freshman. But did that really mean anything?

Not now, Gar thought. Nothing that small meant anything now. He was excited. He couldn't fully understand why. He should have been uneasy, perhaps even a little frightened. He wasn't. He only wished he were smarter so that leading would be easier. He wished he knew more about the reasons his father had for leading the Underground in their town, about why fighting was so necessary and so necessarily undercover.

He believed in his parents' fight. And in what was now his own. But more on faith than knowledge. He felt some little bit of information, perhaps even some small piece of feeling, was missing in him. The words his father used

—freedom, equality, repression, totalitarianism—he knew what they meant. But it was hard for him to understand how they actually touched him.

For he and his family had little enough to complain of. Charlie had been taken from them such a long time ago it was difficult even for Gar to picture him in his own mind. Before then, and since, his father had always been able to provide well for the family. They always had food on their table, shoes on their feet, coats on their shoulders in February.

It was so easy for Elizabeth to get excited. She got positively purple when she talked about health camps, about homogenous communities. What was the word she used? Ghetto, that was it. They were all ghettos hidden under eight happy-sounding syllables, was what she had said. She had been furious when she found out that there had actually been black people in their town when she was small. She wasn't furious because they were there; she was furious because she hadn't known them. And she didn't know any Indians, either, or any Chinese, or any Puerto Ricans or Mexicans. Elizabeth had never, from that day, gotten over the feeling that she had somehow been deprived of something valuable.

Gar didn't know whether he felt deprived of anything or not. That was another difference between Elizabeth and him: Gar was slower in making up his mind. When Elizabeth decided something was right, or that it was right to do something—no matter what—she couldn't be dissuaded. That, Gar decided, was why she had been the leader all the time, and why he had followed.

But all that would have to change now. It would just have to.

D.J. and Gar came around another corner. D.J. nudged

Gar and moved off into some privet. Gar followed, guessing D.J. was approaching his house from behind, carefully. D.J. went a few steps ahead and then stopped, motioning Gar to stay where he was.

D.J. looked through the hedge. His house had a few lights on. In his father's study and in the kitchen, and one on in an upstairs bedroom. But there were no sounds. Everything was still, like a photograph.

He motioned at Gar. "Listen," he whispered, "we'll go up to the garage. The doors are always closed. You lift the door as fast as you can and head back here, fast. I'll start the car as fast as I can and then double back here to pick you up."

Gar said nothing, understanding D.J.'s directions. He followed D.J. through the bushes.

The garage door was closed. Gar stationed himself at its center, tightly gripping the handle. He tensed his body and, when D.J. gave the sign, threw up the door and disappeared around the side of the building, all in seconds.

D.J. streaked into the darkness. He threw open the car door and jumped in, sliding his key into the ignition at the same time. The wheels screeched before the car moved. He did not turn the headlights on.

D.J.'s father had only time to rush out onto the grass on the front lawn and utter a startled "D.J.!" as his son's car shot past him.

D.J. saw his father. He saw him. He felt odd. He felt soft, suddenly. But he grit his teeth.

As the car hit the street pavement and shifted into a forward gear, D.J. heard a siren in the distance. He saw the first beams of the headlights and the first circle of red spinning atop a car at the other end of the road, behind him.

He instantly took his foot off the accelerator so that when he turned the corner toward Gar he wouldn't have to brake—to keep the brake-lights from signaling the car behind him. He wondered briefly whether Chanler was having his father arrested by a Unit, or whether he had simply called the police or the Security Guard. He wondered what exactly the charge would be.

As he slowed down for Gar, he looked at the fuel gauge. There was more than enough gas for the twenty miles to Brookhaven. He wished, though, that he'd thought ahead to fill up before he'd left for school that morning. How far away the morning suddenly seemed.

"We're going back," D.J. said as Gar slammed the car door.

"We can't," Gar said. "There isn't time."

"I'm taking the time," D.J. said defiantly. "I want to see." He swung the car in a U-turn, the headlights still off. The car glided back to the corner, crossed the intersection, and pulled over to the wrong side of the road. D.J. got out.

"Keep the motor running," he said to Gar. "I'll be back in seconds. If I'm not, well—take off!"

D.J. pushed the door to quietly and disappeared into a shadowy yard.

Gar sat behind the wheel of the car, wondering why leading seemed to be so difficult. Obviously, he decided, no one understood yet that he *was* the leader. He hoped he wouldn't have to announce that. He wanted it just to happen.

D.J. ran as quietly as he could to the corner of the lot, hunkering down to look at his house through the stems of the bushes.

A Security Guard's car stood in his driveway. His father

68

was gesturing to the police. Chanler stood behind him, edging him slowly toward the back door of the car.

The scene began to swim before D.J.'s eyes. He turned away.

"Let's go!" he said as he pushed Gar back across the front seat.

12

Walking up the flagstone path, Elizabeth hoped that the little Wheeler boy wasn't *that* little. Or, at least, that his sister was *that* big. What no one needed now was a baby to watch over, to feed and keep happy.

Never Ready stepped up to press a button near the screen door. He was impressed a little by the heavy carved wooden door beyond, but he was too excited to see its detail clearly.

They could hear a bell somewhere inside. Never Ready rang again. They waited. The door was opened.

"Hi," said Freddy, smiling. He wore his bathrobe and pajamas and slippers.

"Hi," said Never Ready. "Is your sister here?"

Freddy's smile faded a little. "I'll see," he said.

Never Ready and Elizabeth were left looking through the screen. After a moment, Freddy returned and held the door open for them.

Elizabeth entered first, looking closely at Freddy, wondering if this boy were the one they had to take. She couldn't see anything seriously wrong. There didn't seem to be anything funny about his feet. And he wasn't that small, after all.

Tank came toward them, looking cautiously out of the corners of her eyes, her head oddly turned half-away from Never Ready. She started to smile but stopped abruptly. "Hello, Anthony," she said.

"Anthony!" echoed Elizabeth, laughing a little.

Tank turned her face to Never Ready, forgetting the pain it cost to smile. Elizabeth gasped.

Never Ready started forward. He understood. Tank had been side-swiped; Chanler had swung out and hit her face along one side, bruising it. There was a huge and bloody bump on the other side of Tank's head, at the forehead, where she had fallen against something. That arm, too, had been hurt somehow in the fall, for it was carefully folded into a sling.

"Julie," Never Ready said softly, "are you all right?"

Tank nodded.

Elizabeth looked carefully. The girl wasn't that much younger than she herself was. The arm wasn't broken. Or maybe there just hadn't been time to set it yet. "Is it broken?" she asked Tank.

"No."

"Good," Elizabeth said, breathing easier. "I'm glad. Listen, could Never Ready and I talk to you a minute, somewhere private?"

Tank looked at Elizabeth, puzzled. She had no idea who Elizabeth was. Still, she nodded and motioned for them to follow her.

Tank lead them into a room where books and broken glass covered the floor, where there were torn curtains and slashed paintings, furniture overturned and blotches of stain on the carpet. Never Ready gasped.

Elizabeth, noting everything but taking no time to speak of it, began immediately. "My name is Elizabeth Bennett," she said. "You know Never Ready. Can you and your brother come with us, right now?"

"Where?" Tank asked, glancing at Freddy who stood watching from a corner.

71

"We're not certain," Elizabeth admitted. "Except for one thing. We're all in danger."

"But how?" Tank wanted to know. "I mean, they've already been here. This afternoon."

Elizabeth frowned. "Did you know," she said sharply, "that whatever is wrong with your brother was discovered?"

Freddy blushed. No one outside the family, except Robin, ever talked about that.

Tank turned to Freddy. Freddy nodded that what Elizabeth said was true. He shuffled a bit and put *that* foot behind the other.

"You think they'll come for him?" Tank asked. "You really think that?"

"We don't know, Julie," Never Ready said. "But D.J. Berryman thinks so. It's just too great a chance to take."

Tank looked at Never Ready and then at Elizabeth. She had a sudden feeling that what they were saying was true, would happen. That all the work she and her parents had done, that all their teaching and caring and efforts would be swept away by a whirring siren and a white truck. She looked at Freddy who was not smiling.

"You'll have to go, Freddy," she said.

Freddy paled.

"No," Elizabeth said. "You both must come. You know best how to take care of him."

"I can't." Tank had not hesitated an instant.

"You must," Elizabeth argued. "Why can't you?"

Tank took a deep breath and cleared her throat. "Because of my mother," she said. "She's dying."

Elizabeth took a step backwards, as though someone had threatened to hit her.

Never Ready sat down and pulled Tank down with

him. He held her hand. He had never done anything like this before. He had no idea what to say.

"Julie," he began, slowly, "Julie, if that's true, we're terribly sorry. We are. But maybe you could think of it this way. Isn't it better for you to say good-bye to her now, when she's alive and when you're alive? When Freddy's here, too. Isn't it better to say good-bye now, without waiting for the . . . the real end? Wouldn't she even maybe want it, want Freddy to get away safely?"

Tank said nothing. She looked at Never Ready. She looked at his hand holding hers. She began to cry. She hadn't cried before. Not all day.

13

"**You have visitors,**" announced Tank's father as he came into the library. His thin figure was jostled and brushed by two shadows that moved past him and into the circle of light.

"Oh no!" Freddy cried, running to his father.

"There, there," said Freddy's father. "What's the matter?"

"I'm afraid it's me, sir," said D.J., trying to smile at the frightened boy. "I was here earlier today."

"You don't mean you—" began Mr. Wheeler, holding Freddy and backing away.

"It's all right, Mr. Wheeler," Elizabeth said, moving forward. "D.J. had to come this afternoon. Right now, he's on the other side.

Tank stood up. "We have to leave, Daddy. Freddy and I," she said. "They know about Freddy's foot."

Mr. Wheeler's look of astonishment did not change.

"Tank," whispered Freddy, peering out from behind his father, "that's the same one."

"I know, I know," said his sister gently. "It's all right, Freddy, really."

"No," persisted Freddy. "I mean the same one that Robin saw."

"Robin who?" asked Gar rather harshly.

Freddy was frightened. He couldn't speak. "A friend of ours," Tank answered. "His house was raided too."

"By you?" Gar asked D.J. D.J. nodded. "Does Chan-

74

ler know you were recognized?" Gar asked. D.J. nodded again.

Elizabeth sighed. That would probably mean seven instead of six.

"Better call him," Gar suggested.

Mr. Wheeler had no idea what all this meant. He opened his mouth to speak, but Tank stopped him. "Come into the kitchen, Daddy. I'll try to explain."

Stunned, her father followed Tank out of the room.

"Robin," Freddy said, not knowing how to put what he wanted to say. "Robin has helped me. He saved me, saved my life. Is he coming with us? Please, can he come with us?" he said, gathering courage enough to look squarely at Gar with the question.

Gar looked back at Freddy, feeling oddly close to the little boy. Without meaning to delve into his memory, he found a cloudy picture of Charlie floating through his mind. "I guess he'll have to, then, won't he?" Gar answered.

Freddy smiled. He went to a side table, picked up the receiver, and dialed. After a moment he spoke. "Is Robin there?" He paused. "Is this Robin Frye's house?" He listened another moment and then held the phone away from his ear.

Gar and Elizabeth and D.J. could hear an odd kind of sound from the receiver. A moaning kind of sound, as though someone were talking through tears and trying to breathe at the same time. Never Ready took the phone from Freddy.

"Hello," he said. "Hello? Could you speak more slowly, please?"

The room was still as Never Ready began to nod. "Yes," he said. "Yes, I see. No. I'm afraid I can't. I'm sorry."

He replaced the phone on its cradle and turned to the

others. "We're too late," Never Ready said. "He's been picked up. That was the maid."

"Where has he gone?" D.J. asked.

"Who took him?" Elizabeth wanted to know.

"She couldn't say," Never Ready answered. "She didn't know much of anything. She was sort of hysterical."

"He's probably at Altoona. That's where they take the men, until there's one of those special trials we hear so much about," Gar said.

"One detention center for men and one for women," Elizabeth added. "But that's at Brookhaven."

"Can we go get him?" Freddy asked quietly of everyone. "He's my friend."

There was a long moment in which no one spoke. Gar focused on D.J., wanting to force him to answer.

After a moment, D.J. shrugged. "I guess we'll have to, won't we?"

Gar felt rewarded. D.J. looked guilty, uncomfortable. But instead of turning back to Gar, D.J. faced Elizabeth instead.

"Freddy," she said, "go upstairs. Say good-night to your mother. Put on some warm clothes and your most comfortable shoes. We'll be doing a lot of travelling."

Freddy smiled, understanding, and moved toward the door, a thin-limbed but chubby-faced little boy ready for bed.

"Jesus!" D.J. said. "What are we going to do with him?"

"Carry him, if we have to," said Gar firmly.

Tank came into the library carrying a wicker basket. She laid it at Never Ready's feet. "I'll be ready in a minute," she said, and turned to follow Freddy up the stairs.

"Where's Altoona?" D.J. asked Elizabeth.

"In the opposite direction from Brookhaven, naturally,"

76

said Elizabeth with a smile. "I wonder if we really can get that other boy out."

"We have to try," Gar said. "No matter how tricky it is."

"We saw Altoona once. Remember, Gar?" Elizabeth said. "All white with trenches dug in circles around it."

"Trenches?" D.J. said. "What for?"

"It's some sort of security system, I guess," Gar answered. "No one ever breaks out of Altoona."

"That's mostly because they're not there very long," added his sister.

D.J. shuddered. "You don't mean—"

"No," Elizabeth said. "Nothing quite that horrible. It's only a way station, between being arrested and being sent to a real prison with chains and bars and dogs."

"But what about your parents?" asked D.J. "What about getting to Brookhaven?"

"Obviously," Gar said, "that will have to wait."

"Right," Elizabeth agreed. "No one will expect us to double back anyway."

Gar cleared his throat. "D.J." he said, "there's something else."

"What?"

"Altoona's where they'll take your father, too."

"We're ready," called Tank from the doorway.

Elizabeth turned to see Mr. Wheeler standing between his two children, his arms on their shoulders. His face seemed pale but he was trying to smile. He nodded at them all, and at no one in particular. "They're ready now," he said softly. "They've said their good-byes."

Never Ready saw Tank had been crying again. He started to go to her but Elizabeth held him back. Instead, she went to Tank's side and put her arm around Tank's shoulder. Together they started out of the house to D.J.'s car.

14

Even though there were only ten minutes to go until curfew, the group took extra care settling into D.J.'s car. Tank, with her right arm in the sling, sat in the back seat, behind D.J., with Freddy between her and Never Ready. Elizabeth squeezed in between D.J. and her brother in front. It was decided to keep the supplies inside the car rather than to put them in the trunk where, in an emergency, they might not be available.

"All aboard!" called Never Ready softly as the motor turned over.

Elizabeth took a big breath loudly and held it. "What's that for?" asked Gar.

"I'm going under," Elizabeth answered. "Underground, underwater. I'm planning to stay down as long as Wagenson stays on top where he is now."

"Which way?" asked D.J.

"Head right, down Grand Avenue," Elizabeth answered. "Better use your lights, too. The Security Guards would only stop a dark car moving through town."

D.J. pulled on his lights and drove law-abidingly through the streets. He wished again he knew more about the countryside.

"Elizabeth," Gar said quietly to his sister, "maybe you better tell D.J. where Altoona is. Just in case."

Elizabeth nodded. "It's easy. Head first for the Capitol Building. Then, however you can, go directly west from

78

there. About ten or twelve miles out there's a river. We follow that south until we can see Perry. Then, as soon as we can, we cross the river and head west again. Ten more miles or so and we're there."

D.J. listened carefully, trying to picture the movements Elizabeth mentioned.

"Everyone all right back there?" Gar asked.

Never Ready smiled to himself. His arm was across the seat and touching Tank's shoulder lightly. "Couldn't be better," he answered.

"It's all white and has trenches?" D.J. asked under his breath.

"And surrounded by absolutely nothing," Elizabeth said. "Just sits out there on the plain and attracts sunlight. It must be hell in summer."

"How many people do you think are there?" asked D.J.

"We only saw it once," Gar answered. "There's a road that runs along some bluffs about four miles away. We looked down at it, and the building just sort of wavered in the sun. I'd guess maybe it could take a couple hundred people."

A Security Guard's van crossed an intersection ahead. D.J. slowed at first and then pressed on, looking down the street to follow the wagon's lights. He turned in an opposite direction and drove for a few blocks before realigning himself with the top of the Capitol, lit in the distance.

"Do you think we'll be all right?" Tank leaned forward and put her chin on the seat ahead of her. "I mean, won't our families be questioned?"

"Probably," said Gar. "They don't know anything, though."

79

"My guess is," said D.J. comfortingly, "that Chanler or whoever is investigating will realize that after a while, and give up."

"Won't your car be chased?" Tank asked worriedly. "They'll have a bulletin out for it."

"She's right, D.J.," said Gar. "We can't exit on an ordinary road. Even your permit number will be listed."

The six rode a few moments in silence. D.J. guided the car around the Capitol Circle and headed west, as Elizabeth had directed. They entered a neighborhood familiar only to D.J. He remembered a raid there. An old woman.

The buildings they passed were farther and farther apart. Occasionally several shamble-down houses stood together, as though for comfort against the night. Few lights shone from windows they passed. They were approaching the city limits.

Tank, feeling slightly reassured, stopped worrying about herself and Freddy and the others. A new thought had entered her head. She had wept when she said good-bye to her mother. But what she worried most about, she suddenly realized, was her father. If she and Freddy were still gone when their mother died, who would he have to turn to? How terrible it would be for him to be alone. She wondered if she should write him and tell him she loved him and not to be too unhappy. But perhaps the mail would be opened.

The car rolled slowly to a halt at a stop sign. Another sign, directly ahead, told them they must turn either right or left. They could go no farther.

D.J. made a U-turn and started back the way he had come. No one spoke; they waited for an explanation.

The car slipped quietly into a dirt lane. D.J. turned the motor and the lights off at the same time. He leaned back and breathed deeply. They were out after curfew now.

He swung around in his seat so he could look at everyone in the car. He smiled as he saw Freddy, sound asleep and leaning confidently against Never Ready's shoulder. Never Ready smiled back.

"Well," D.J. said.

"That wasn't so bad," said Tank, smiling a little for the first time since leaving her home. "Do we open the baskets now?"

"You're leaving the car here," Elizabeth guessed.

"No," D.J. answered. "That would be too easy. Someone would find it and know exactly where we were headed."

"What then?" asked Gar.

"We'll try a couple hours of sleep," D.J. said. "Then you and Elizabeth take the others and head into that field ahead. Just go straight for, say, maybe twenty or twenty-five minutes. It won't be hard walking. You can see even from here it's pretty level. And there are enough trees should anything happen."

"What about you?" Never Ready asked.

"I'll take the car back a little, and head it in another direction. Then I'll double back along this road. I'll catch up. I should be able to join you not much more than an hour after you stop."

The six people were quiet. Freddy's easy breathing and a few night birds scavenging were the only sounds heard.

"We have to walk all the way?" said Tank.

"I'm afraid so," D.J. answered. "We're going to be doing a lot of walking from now on. It's safer. And it's safer still walking in the dark."

"But what about Freddy?" Tank whispered.

81

"He's got you and us," Gar answered gently.

"And at least he's wearing trousers," Elizabeth joked, pulling her own skirt closely around her.

Tank sat back, not relaxed. Never Ready's hand touched her shoulder. She tried to feel better.

Again all was quiet. But the quiet was heavy with waiting; the idea of sleep was impossible for everyone but Freddy.

"Let's get going," Gar said finally. "If we're going to move at night, the more night we have the better."

"Yes," Never Ready agreed. "It's better to start now."

D.J. looked to Elizabeth. She nodded agreement.

D.J. started the car again. Tank nudged Freddy awake. D.J. drove carefully to the end of the road and stopped. He left the motor running and the lights off. Saying good-bye to no one, the five passengers got out of the car. Doors were slammed as quietly as possible and feet padded carefully across the gravel. When D.J. could no longer hear footsteps, when the shadows he watched had disappeared into other, bigger and darker outlines, he made another U-turn and drove away.

15

D.J. saw a Security Van cross the road directly ahead of him. Quickly he turned into the nearest driveway, as though he were coming home. The van rolled on without slowing.

Looking back, D.J. was surprised to see still another van, red lights circling above it but with no siren blaring, heading in the same direction as the first but travelling a slightly different route.

He understood then. The alert was on. The guards were being directed to every access to the city. They would be waiting at every entrance and exit post. For his car, for him.

D.J. backed out of the drive and continued, moving away from the dirt crossing where the group had left him. He spotted a driveway that was nearly hidden by trees and bushes growing along its boundaries. He swung the car in and turned off the motor. He sat still, listening.

It was a good place, he decided. The house appeared abandoned. The car could scarcely be seen from the road even in the daytime. It would take Chanler and his crew several days to find.

If it takes twenty minutes to walk a mile quickly, D.J. reasoned, he should be able to make better time by running, walking, running. He looked at his speedometer. He had driven nearly four miles from the crossroad. He should be able to do a mile every ten minutes. Forty minutes and he would be off the road, into the field. He could certainly travel faster across the countryside as one man than five people could together. His timing was almost perfect. He was pleased.

He got out of the car quickly, and locked its doors. At a run, he started back along the roadway. He ran, counting two hundred to himself, and walked, counting one hundred. He was not unhappy. He enjoyed running. He had enjoyed running in school and was probably the best half-miler Roosevelt High had had in many years.

The only thing that spoiled his pleasure was what his mind sang along with each step. "Robin Frye and Father, Robin Frye and Father, Robin Frye and Father." He knew he had to get Frye out, if it was possible in any way. But he hadn't made up his mind about his old man. If he *were* in Altoona, what would D.J. have to do?

Two hundred, one hundred, two hundred. It wasn't so hard. He increased his speed to three hundred, one hundred, three hundred. Once he crossed an intersection as a Security Van swung around the corner behind him. He threw himself onto the grass at the roadside and held his breath, his heart pumping from his exercise and sounding so loudly in his ears that he thought anyone within three miles distance could hear it. The van rolled by, its warning lights circling above his head, the officers inside looking well above his prone body.

Two or three deep breaths and he was up again, running. Three hundred, one hundred, three hundred.

What would his mother feel, he wondered, with his father arrested and jailed? Probably, he thought, at first pleased and then sorry, worried for him. D.J. suspected his mother still loved his father, in spite of herself, in spite of everything. That was probably why she had stayed away ever since that time. She could have faced him and his father if she hadn't loved them.

Three hundred, one hundred.

In less than an hour, D.J. was back where he had begun, vaulting over the dead-end sign and landing in dirt and plowed-under potatoes. Ducking as he ran, he continued straight ahead along a furrow. The moon had been hidden. Now a round slice edged out from behind a cloud. He felt horribly visible.

He saw a stand of trees ahead. They could be bordering the field, edging one piece of property from another, or—he could almost feel the icy water around his waist —they could be lining a river or a creek. He couldn't slow his pace. He drove directly into them. He heard his breath alternating with his footfalls. He could not hear any rushing water.

Relieved, he ran on. Three hundred, one hundred, three hundr—"D.J.!" D.J. stopped and threw himself down. He held his breath. "D.J.!" someone half-called, half-whispered again. It was Gar. "Over here!"

D.J. rose and followed the voice. He sank down, exhausted suddenly, next to Elizabeth. He smiled. Everyone smiled back. So far, so good.

"How far do you think we've come?" he panted to Gar.

"I make it maybe one and a half, maybe two miles. We really burned up the turf."

D.J. looked quickly around for Freddy, who smiled at him and said, "I'm O.K. Gar and I really flew."

"We went a little farther than you said to," Elizabeth said. "We wanted to wait until we got to some kind of natural cover."

D.J. nodded as Never Ready handed him a canteen of water. D.J. allowed himself only one swallow and

85

handed it back. "Well," he said waiting another moment for his breath to come more easily, "we'd better get under way. The farther we go tonight, the less we have to do tomorrow."

They rose and arranged themselves in file. Gar led, D.J. and Never Ready followed, each holding one of Freddy's arms to lift him over difficult obstacles. Tank followed, and Elizabeth was only a step behind.

Gar began to feel comfortable as he led the group. The only thought that disturbed him, made him a little angry even, was that he felt somehow as though he were being allowed to *play* the leader. That Elizabeth and D.J. had silently agreed to let Gar have his head for a while, until something really important happened. *Still,* Gar thought, *I've got a lot of muscle. I won't give up easily.*

Crunching through underbrush and slicing through weed patches kept Never Ready alert. He liked holding onto Freddy's hand. It made him feel closer to Tank. He hoped she noticed how gentle he was with Freddy. He hoped she would come to see him as a protector, as a . . . . Even in the dark Never Ready blushed. He would have to control *that* kind of thought.

Behind D.J., who carried their provisions, Tank moved easily enough. Only occasionally did she favor her arm as she ducked under a branch or stepped gingerly across a rocky hummock. And, from time to time, she looked up to see how Freddy was doing. She could not help but notice Never Ready's aid.

Elizabeth said nothing, following Tank, bringing up the rear, looking behind every once in a while to scan the horizon for signs of pursuing lights.

Once D.J. nearly stopped dead, forcing Tank to look

up quickly and step around him for fear of a collision. He wanted to ask Elizabeth something. He had just realized, he had allowed himself to remember, that the group had no plan, neither of destination beyond Altoona nor of breaking into the prison for Robin Frye. They had no tools, no weapons; he wondered if they even had enough food for the journey.

But he submerged these thoughts determinedly. He realized, too, that dwelling on them now would only dishearten the group. He suspected, anyway, that Elizabeth knew everything he did. What could she have said that was real or honest? Except that something might turn up?

Miraculously, by four in the morning, they had reached the stream Elizabeth had mentioned before. They climbed the hills that ran along one side of it, the side closest the town they had fled. Gar had thought it best to stay on the highest ground possible; there was more cover, there was more opportunity to see approaching danger.

As the sun peeked over the city behind them, they halted. Nestled in a grove of pine and cottonwood, deep in grass and bushes, they couldn't be seen from above; they wouldn't be seen from below.

Freddy and Tank fell asleep instantly, leaning together for warmth and security. Never Ready watched them parentally for a while, and then lay down within a few feet of Tank. Gar and D.J. and Elizabeth arranged themselves on three sides of the others, leaving only the river side behind them unwatched.

D.J.'s breathing soon was even and quiet. Gar tossed a bit, occasionally leaning up on an elbow to look at his little band, then lying back down, trying for a comfortable position amid pebbles and pine cones. Elizabeth sat facing the city, watching the sun rise. Saying good-bye again to her parents. Remembering the night's run. Wondering what lay ahead.

A bird feeding in the underbrush startled her. Elizabeth turned away from the sun to look for the chirping diner. At first she saw nothing. But her eyes wandered a bit more widely and there, in the distance, coming across the same fields she had come, was a tiny caravan. Its head-lights were still on in the hazy light of dawn. She guessed it was perhaps two miles away, and well upstream from where they had stopped to sleep.

Could Chanler have gotten organized so quickly, she wondered. If so, he was heading in the direction he assumed D.J. would travel, being guided probably by where D.J. had left his car.

For a moment, Elizabeth wasn't certain what she should do. Should she wake everyone? Should they begin to move again amongst the cover and darkness of the undergrowth? No. Everyone was tired. And after all, if it was Chanler, there was still a fifty-fifty chance he would turn north instead of south when he reached the river. There would be no signs or tracks where his motor-cade would halt. He would only be guessing. There was still time.

She closed her eyes. She meant to stay awake. She thought someone should be on the alert, just in case. But the night's dash and the tension of the day before had worn her out. Within minutes her head fell forward and she was asleep, leaning like a ragdoll against the trunk of an old tree.

She had not seen, nor felt, the pair of dark brown eyes that watched her from not more than fifty feet down the slope.

F
N4822

16

No one slept late. Even with the trees as natural cover, the sun broke too warmly through. The baskets were opened and small portions of provisions were passed about. As the night before, no one wanted to wait until it was dark to begin moving.

Elizabeth again brought up the rear of the column, gladly. No one was conscious of her frequent looks behind, attempts to see if the caravan still followed them or had turned north. She struggled with her suspicion but said nothing.

Gar led most of the way, occasionally taking one of Freddy Wheeler's arms or a basket from D.J. or Never Ready. Tank plowed after, quiet and careful of her arm. She said it felt better, but no one allowed her to take it out of the sling. There was no point in taking chances unless one absolutely had to.

Freddy seemed to be holding his own, until the group stopped for water or, late in the day, for lunch. Then he huddled into himself and clenched his teeth, the pain somehow seeming to grow sharper when he took his weight *off* the foot than when he was walking on it. He never admitted his discomfort to anyone. He didn't have to.

Below the six, another figure kept pace. Moving cautiously and as silently as possible, stopping when they stopped and starting at the same time, hidden and

89

12,935

stealthy. From time to time, it too halted to look behind for the caravan. A hand reached out to take autumn berries as the form moved through the underbrush. A nearly inaudible sigh answered the rests called from above.

By twilight, the six had walked down-river nearly far enough to see the small town of Perry in the distance. It was Gar who, straightening up after ducking beneath some overhanging sumac, saw its outlines. He smiled to himself and turned to tell the others.

They decided then to rest. They had walked nearly eight hours with only five stops during the day. They could sleep during early evening, getting underway once more at midnight. Gar volunteered first to search out a crossing in the river below. They would have to turn west again that night.

By the time Gar had struggled back up the hillside to where the others were, all but Elizabeth had fallen into deep, dreamless sleep. "It looks O.K.," he said to his sister as he sank down beside her. "A few tricky rocks that may give Freddy trouble. But I think we can handle that." He smiled tiredly at Elizabeth and lay on his back, his arm covering his eyes to keep out the last of the day's light. Elizabeth smiled at him in response, and looked off again into the distance. She was waiting for darkness to tell her what so far that day she had been unable to find out: was Chanler behind them, or miles to the north?

Dusk fell easily across the midwestern fields. Trees grew darker and taller before one's eyes and melded into the night-black air. Crickets scraped occasionally, and jays rushed about, gathering the last of their day's insect requirement. A squirrel moved softly above Elizabeth and ran down a tree trunk to stand sentinel-like, watching her. Idly she waved at him and he turned tail, disappearing into tall grass.

Twenty feet below Elizabeth, hidden by an overhanging boulder, other eyes watched as the squirrel slid down the hillside and investigated an odd pile of debris. No hand was raised in greeting. The squirrel took what it wanted and disappeared again, moving across the hillside and out of sight. The figure resting below the rock sighed and wondered what squirrel would taste like. So far it hadn't been necessary.

Elizabeth suddenly stood. To the north she saw what she had hoped she wouldn't: headlights. Three cars. Moving slowly along the bottom of the hillside that bordered the river.

She bent down to shake Gar awake and then stopped. It wouldn't do any good to wake people and run. The cars in the distance were moving too steadily and too quickly to outrun forever.

Hardly seeming to think, Elizabeth started to move away from the camp. When she was fifty feet away she began trotting, and soon she was running as fast as she could, ducking under branches, diving through gorse and thistle, slipping as she twisted an ankle on some rocks. But her direction was certain; her determination unbreakable.

The figure below, hearing the scuffle of footsteps above, followed. At a distance, though, for what the girl ahead seemed to be doing was unclear.

Elizabeth stopped only a few times to breathe deeply and lean against a friendly tree. Her eyes never left the horizon. Running again, she let herself drift downwards, toward the city side of the hill. She maintained her pace for nearly an hour and then began to climb back up the hillside until she was running along its peak. She slowed her pace and began picking up small twigs and branches of trees as she walked. Finally, winded but secure in what she was doing, Elizabeth sank down and began shaping a mound of wood on the slope.

Below her she could hear the river easing through rock and driftwood. The moon, which was bright and nearly full, gave her light to work. She checked distances. She mentally drew sight lines. She pulled a box of matches from her pocket and lit one, touching it gently to the tinder she had collected.

Elizabeth smiled as the flames grew, as she saw her feet and her hands lit by the light from the fire. She became aware suddenly that the night, after all, had a chill in it. She was grateful for the fire's warmth.

Looking down and into the short distance, she saw the lights of the caravan. For a moment she was terribly afraid. Afraid it had all been too late, in vain. But then the lights stopped. After a few minutes, all three cars turned and began coming toward her. The flames threatened to die. Elizabeth stood and gathered whatever loose wood there was around her to put on the fire. Then she sat down again.

At least at Brookhaven she would be closer to her parents. Maybe she could get a message through to them. If the Resistance had begun seriously at last, there would be *someone* in the detention center who would know how to do it.

Anyway, she thought dreamily, watching the lights in the distance grow clearer and larger, the others will have more time. Maybe, and Elizabeth smiled thinking about it, maybe someday Gar and D.J. would hit Brookhaven, too, for her. Wouldn't that be marvelous! To be free again!

But if she were no longer there? Suppose she had already been tried and transferred somewhere else?

But that was a possibility she didn't want to consider. Not now.

Hypnotized by the approaching headlights that had started at last to climb the hillside toward her, and finally afraid a little, Elizabeth did not hear the footsteps behind her, retreating, beginning to run without thought for noise or caution.

17

Frannie Heffernan threw her bulky body through the remaining yards of weed and sapling, and burst into the circle of sleeping forms with both arms reaching out, bending and straightening as she grabbed at each person. She charged from Gar to D.J. to Tank and Freddy. Never Ready sat bolt upright on the grass trying to see.

Frannie stopped a moment to get her breath. "You've been given a reprieve," she said finally. "Time to hit the road."

"Who are you?" D.J. asked, on his feet and buttoning his jacket against a chilly breeze that had snuck through the trees atop the hill. "What's going on?"

"There's no time to explain," Frannie said impatiently, still breathing hard. "Which way were you headed?"

Never Ready still couldn't see what the speaker's face looked like. It was too dark. All he could see were eyes and occasionally a set of teeth. He reached in a basket nearby and picked up a candle and matches. He struck one match and tried to light the candle but the wind extinguished it quickly. He had seen, nonetheless.

"How'd you get here?" Never Ready gasped. "How'd you get out?"

"Oh God," Frannie sighed dramatically. "Listen, chief, I'll answer any question you can think of—later. Right now you'd just better come with me."

"D.J.!" Gar called suddenly. "Elizabeth's gone!"

"She sure is, boy." Frannie said. "You're damned lucky she is, too. Otherwise you'd all be gone. Or goners."

"Elizabeth!" Gar shouted into the night. "Elizab—!"

Frannie threw herself the few feet that separated her from Gar and covered his mouth with her hand. "Boy!" she said, "you ain't got the sense you was born with! That's the surest way I know to join her."

D.J. was fully awake now. "Maybe you could take a second to explain," he said calmly, but with a definite edge to his voice. "If it's not too much trouble."

Frannie took her hand from Gar's mouth and faced D.J. "My Daddy was right," she said. "You white folk sure are defensive."

Freddy, the last to awake, gasped. What he had thought was true, was. Frannie heard him and turned to face him. But she was smiling. "What's the matter, chile," she asked. "Ain't you never seen no niggers before?"

Freddy smiled back, as usual. "No, ma'am," he said.

"You can cut out the dialect," D.J. said.

"Ah jes' don' wanna disappoint no one," Frannie answered. "Ah mean, we got our place and you got yours."

Never Ready coughed, a little embarrassed. "Listen," he said, "if this is supposed to be the time for hitting the road, tell us why and let's get going."

"Right!" Frannie said. "A sensible man, at last."

"Where's my sister?" Gar asked.

"Riding in a big black security car," Frannie told him. "There are three of them, all strung out, heading for the city. She saw them following, doubled back and lit a fire. She begged them to come get her. They did."

"How do you know?" Gar demanded.

"I followed her," Frannie said quietly. "I've been fol-

95

lowing all of you. It beats picking blackberries."

"But you're supposed to be in your own community, with—" D.J. began.

"I know, *I know,*" Frannie cut him off. "But I couldn't stand it any longer. Anything beats that kind of life. I took off a couple of weeks ago. Came past Omaha and past Altoona, headed toward your town, when we crossed trails. It's good to have someone to talk to. I've been running for days."

"Do we have to run now?" asked Tank. "Are they chasing us now?"

"Whoever's tailing you ain't too smart, either. This man's sister must have figured that out in advance. My guess is that she'll be questioned back in town instead of out here on the road, where they could turn around and scoop you all up if they wanted. But I wouldn't waste any more time."

"We were going to Altoona," Never Ready said.

"Then let's get going." Frannie replied. "Travelling by night's safer. Maybe we can make Raph's by tomorrow night."

"Who's Raph?" D.J. asked.

"Never you mind," Frannie said with a smile. "Just get up on your feet and move."

Tank reached down for Freddy's hand. She was sorry to lose Elizabeth. But now, with this—. "Say," Tank asked, "what's your name, anyway?"

"Frannie Heffernan," came the answer. "Black, beautiful, buxom and brilliant."

Freddy laughed at the way Frannie spoke. He wasn't certain he knew exactly what she said.

"I'm going after Elizabeth," Gar said suddenly.

96

"That's ridiculous, man," Frannie told him. "Your sister's riding in comfort twenty miles away by now. There's nothing you can do."

"She's right," D.J. said. "You're better off with us than alone, anyway."

"Maybe they won't hurt her," Tank offered.

"They couldn't," Gar answered, feeling doubt but hiding it. "Elizabeth's got more guts than anybody I ever knew."

"O.K.," Frannie said. "That's that. Let's go!"

Gar hesitated. He had a feeling he was losing something, but he wasn't sure what it was. He felt suddenly at sea. Without Elizabeth near him, he felt empty. "There's a good crossing down there," he finally said, without real strength to his voice. He pointed at the edge of the hill toward the river.

"Probably is," Frannie said, "but there's an easier one over this way. I've only crossed the river four times in the last few days."

Gar looked at Frannie a moment, and shrugged, giving up. D.J. looked at her, too. He'd never before really had contact with any of "those people," as his father called them. He'd always assumed they had simply lived lives much like his own, only somewhere else. He knew he was supposed to feel something, supposed to feel something unpleasant. He wasn't at all certain he did.

"Terrific," D.J. said at last, when no one had begun to move. "Five fugitives too sleepy and too tired to move, and one black Daniel Boone."

"You bet your ass, boy," Frannie retorted happily, lunging off toward the river, feeling she would be followed, now that the talking had come to an end.

97

D.J. started down the hill after Frannie. Tank and Never Ready walked on either side of Freddy, helping him down easily and securely. Gar brought up the rear, standing on the hill's crest before following, thinking about his sister. Now there were two reasons for doubling back to Brookhaven. He made a silent vow to Elizabeth.

The six made their way quickly and with few accidents down the hillside to the river's edge. Frannie pointed out the crossing and said she would lead, since she'd crossed there before. She stepped out onto a flat rock that was washed by the stream, making it slippery and shiny even though the moon had disappeared over the hill. She stood a moment, half-turned, as if to say that the feat could be performed, and then she stepped out toward another boulder.

D.J. followed her, and then Tank and Never Ready. Gar picked up Freddy when his turn came and, precariously balanced, started across.

Near the opposite bank, wet from the few steps that had had to be taken through the water at one point, Frannie turned to see the group's progress. There were only a few feet more to go and luckily there was a fat log sticking out into the water from the bank ahead.

Satisfied all was well, Frannie jauntily took a step and then another.

"Land o'Goshen!" came her shout. "Lawsy!"

Frannie started to laugh. A full sound, not loud, seemed to shake her big frame and made her seem to be bouncing in and out of the water where she sat.

D.J. leaned down to help her to her feet. "Shhh!" he cautioned, smiling at her.

"For all my shouting up top," Frannie said, "I just can't get used to the idea that danger's not funny." She

98

chuckled a minute more to herself. "I mean, just a little," she added.

"My name is Daniel J. Berryman. D.J.," said D.J. as he and Frannie stepped onto the grass.

"Well, good," Frannie said. "I'm glad you told me. Finally. What about them?" she asked, pointing as the others made their way to shore. D.J. told her.

"Are you hurt?" Tank asked solicitously.

"No, thanks," Frannie answered. "Just due for a little dose of walking pneumonia. Let's march, gang."

Frannie accepted D.J.'s jacket as they started westwards again, ducking branches and stepping around puddles, holding shrubbery back for each other and beginning to hit a measured pace. Tank could hear D.J. explaining to Frannie why they were on the run. Frannie asked short, direct questions. D.J. answered each one without extra words.

Tank thought again about Elizabeth. She wondered if she ever would have had the courage to do what Elizabeth did. She would miss Elizabeth, really. For Elizabeth had made Tank feel not quite so ungainly, not quite so far away from being a real, human person. For someone she hadn't known long, Tank had the feeling that Elizabeth and she could have been good friends.

Yet here was this other girl, Frannie Heffernan. And black! Tank smiled a little to herself. She couldn't remember ever seeing someone like this before, although, unlike Freddy, she would never have admitted it. Why, the blacks must have moved into their own towns more than ten years ago, when she was still almost a baby. But here Frannie was, all round and clever, striding out ahead in slacks and sneakers that were still dripping.

"Tank?" Freddy called softly.

Tank looked around. "What?" she said, almost forgetting to duck around a bramble bush in the path as the others had done.

"She's neat, isn't she?" Freddy said.

Tank nodded. "Do you like her?" she asked quietly, so as not to be overheard.

"Except when she talks that funny way," Freddy said. "Why does she do that?"

"You'll have to ask her, Freddy," Tank answered. "I'm not really sure." But in the back of her mind, surfacing slowly, an explanation began to present itself to Tank.

She put her memories aside. They were only half-heard things, anyway. Maybe later she and Frannie could talk about those things. Right now, Tank decided, it was enough to have Frannie along. She made Tank feel better about everything, even about losing Elizabeth.

For Frannie seemed to know exactly what she was doing. She had taken over. Tank was glad. She guessed Frannie wasn't more than a year or two older, at most, than she was. Beside her, Tank felt suddenly slimmer, closer to being the Julie Wheeler of her dreams.

Tank laughed softly to herself. Color didn't make any difference. But size did.

18

"**Oh no!**" cried Tank as she fell forward, dragging Freddy with her into damp leaves, sticks, and gravel.

For one minute too many, Tank had been dreaming. It was nearly three in the morning. The six had been moving steadily through fields and thickets for several hours. Tank has stopped concentrating some yards back. She had forgotten about direction and speed and caution. She had been thinking about Julie Wheeler. And about Anthony John Newman, III.

Freddy bounded up, unharmed. He stood looking down at his sister. Tank held her damaged arm up farther than the sling did, as though by doing so the pain would lessen.

Gar came up to them. "Are you all right?" he asked, bending down. He used his bulk to lift Tank to her feet.

"I guess so," Tank said quietly. She looked nervously ahead, aware that she must not hold up the march any longer than was necessary.

D.J., Frannie, and Never Ready—hearing no footsteps behind them—stopped, turned, and walked back through the dark.

"Now what?" D.J. asked.

"It's nothing," Tank apologized. "I tripped."

"Oh well," Frannie sighed, letting herself sink onto the ground, "we may as well stop a while, anyway. We can't make Raph's tonight in any case."

Never Ready was relieved. "Let's build a fire," he said.

"It's colder than it should be at this time of year." He started off to collect what wood he could see by the faint light from above.

"Hold it!" Frannie commanded. Never Ready did. "No fire," she said definitely. "Not for a while yet, anyway."

"But why not?" Never Ready asked.

"My friend," Frannie said, as though explaining the simplest thing to an idiot, "there are only two times of day when you can light a *match* and feel fairly safe about it! At dawn. And at dusk. When the light is dim and smoky all by itself. A fire now would be seen for miles."

D.J. smiled. "Well and good," said he, "but I remember reading that if you sit down and rest, and maybe fall asleep, when it's this cold, you could freeze to death."

"Honey," Frannie said, "you just try it! No way! I'm a hundred and sixty pounds of solid, warm and beautiful blackness. I'm the best blanket *you'll* ever have!"

Gar hunkered down. So did Freddy. "We could eat something," Never Ready suggested.

"How much stuff have we got left?" D.J. asked.

"Not much," answered Tank. "I guess we didn't bring the right things." She opened first the basket and then the canvas bag. "Crackers, two chocolate bars, some asparagus soup. And a box of Band-Aids."

No one spoke. The list wasn't appetizing. It didn't sound like food at all.

In the dark, Gar sat trying to remember how long exactly they had been away from their homes. Everything had happened so fast. Everything seemed to flow into and out of everything else. One day they had tried to kidnap Chanler and had failed, eventually, when it counted most. They had fled. Across the countryside for one entire, breathtakingly hot day, and then, their

102

second night, Elizabeth had disappeared. Now, on their third night out, Gar had a feeling that everyone was ready to sink into the ground and sleep for days, gathering whatever dust or rain fell upon them, getting moldy and brown, melting into the leaves and tree trunks that surrounded them.

"Now, children," Frannie said, breaking into the moment, "you just go right ahead and eat anything your little hearts desire. We'll have berries for lunch. Later, tomorrow night, if you can hang on, maybe we'll have pancakes and cakes and bread."

"We don't have any of those things," reminded Freddy.

"But we just might," Frannie said. "Wait and see."

Tank moved in between Frannie and D.J. "I'm tired," she said. "Maybe we should get some sleep."

"I'm not sleepy," Freddy complained.

"I am," Gar said.

"You're sure we couldn't build a fire?" asked Never Ready.

"Boy," Frannie said, *"you* can build any old fire you want. You just walk back a couple of miles first."

The six sat huddled together. The wind blew over their heads. Tank leaned against Never Ready and felt warmed. D.J. picked up a corner of his jacket from Frannie's shoulders and put it around his own. "Any old campfire songs will do," he said with a smile.

"Or a ghost story," chimed in Freddy.

"Maybe just a chorus or two of 'Swing Low, Sweet Chariot,' " chuckled Frannie. "Or 'Old Black Joe.' "

"How about that new, all-time favorite, Old Black Frannie?" D.J. suggested.

"You do catch on, boy," Frannie laughed. "What would you like to know?"

103

"Who you are," said Gar.

"Where you came from," Tank suggested.

"What kind of life you had there," Never Ready added.

"Ahh, the old Life-and-Times bit," Frannie mused. "Tell you what. I'll talk a while. But when the last one of you drifts off to sleepy-time, I'll shut up. I won't ever say another word about any of it."

"Blackmail," D.J. noted. Frannie nodded.

Everyone tried to get comfortable.

"Well," began Frannie, "first off, I come from a family of troublemakers." She smiled to herself. "At least that's what our Mr. Wagenson would say. Only he'd probably say it nastier.

"It started with my Daddy and my uncle. A long time ago, when black people were all supposed to be poor and living in dirt, my Daddy and his brother just started to make money. Not a whole lot, mind you. Nothing like millions. But more than people thought a black man should. To make matters worse, they hustled enough together to send a cousin of mine to what used to be called college."

"Maturity Centers, you mean," corrected D.J.

"Right," Frannie said. "That's what they are now. Back then, it was something else. Anyway, my cousin Joanna made a mistake, too. She got to be smart. I mean, she was smarter than most people thought black people should be. She even got on television. That's when the real trouble began. I mean, that's how come our whole family got to be marked."

"How?" Gar asked.

"She got on television with a guy named Agnew. He was a sort of vice-president then."

"Ohhh," Tank said. "So that's who he was."

"That's who he was," nodded Frannie. "Of course, I was a baby then. I don't remember any of this myself, just what my Daddy told me. But it seems my cousin made Mr. Agnew look pretty foolish. I imagine it wasn't as hard as all that."

"What happened?" D.J. asked.

"Just that," Frannie said. "From that very moment, our whole family was marked and set down to be first. Or among the first. In those days, like now, the Government had all kinds of lists in Washington. You know, people against the war. People belonging to other parties. People they didn't like. Well, we got to be right up there, at the head of the list of people they didn't like."

Frannie shook her head, thinking to herself. "So when Wagenson comes along," she continued, "all he has to do is open the files and pull out the names. Ours jumped right up and shouted at him. He didn't even wait to start this homogenous community stuff. He just hauled my Daddy and Uncle Fred away to be 'investigated.' When he found out they didn't know half as much as my cousin, he let them go and went after Joanna." A sudden note of sadness entered Frannie's voice. "We haven't seen her since, not to this very day."

"But where is she?" asked Tank. "People don't just disappear."

"That's what we said, too, honey, but we were wrong. People *do* just disappear. They didn't used to, but they do now. Why, nearly every day somebody just presses her own left wrist and becomes invisible."

"Really?" gasped Freddy.

Frannie smiled at him. "No, Freddy, I'm only kidding. What I mean is that the Government has ways of making people seem to disappear. They arrest them."

105

"Oh," said Freddy.

"Oh, indeed," Frannie echoed. "Anyway, Joanna got separated from her husband, and from her little boy. And that was that."

"Why didn't you fight?" Gar asked. "Or organize, or do something?"

"That, honey, is the question of all time," Frannie said. "Even for me it's hard to understand. I guess people weren't sure who it was they were supposed to fight. The Government maybe. Their long-haired kids. Teachers. The Russians. No one seemed to know what to do first, my Daddy said. So what happened was that nobody fought. No one did anything. People just decided that if something happened that didn't happen to them, it wasn't any of their business. They didn't want to be involved. They probably didn't even know how to be involved. And they weren't taking any chances. It wasn't just black people who were lazy. It was everybody."

"You should have fought," Gar said softly.

Frannie nodded agreement. "Still," she said, "no one did. And no one had a chance to later, when this homogenous shit came up."

"What?" Freddy asked.

"When the President decided to set up homogenous communities," Frannie explained. "Places for people other than white people to live."

"How did it happen?" Never Ready asked.

"Well," said Frannie, "you'll just have to take my word for it. I mean, probably none of us here can remember, unless it would be you, D.J. But my Daddy remembered."

"What did he say?" D.J. asked.

"It was simple," Frannie replied. "What Wagenson did was to do it first and explain why he did it afterwards."

106

Frannie took a big breath and shifted around, trying to get comfortable by crossing her legs and laying them across Never Ready's.

After a minute, she spoke again. "In the old days a lot of different kinds of people lived in the cities. Mostly, they lived in little knots. All the black people would live in one place; all the Italians somewhere else. Like that. Anyway, just like today only maybe worse, there was a lot of crime. You know, riots and looting and shouting and all. Pretty soon, it was the people who lived in those little knots that everyone suspected."

"Why?" Never Ready wanted to know.

"Who knows?" Frannie said. "It was easy, I guess. And someone had to be to blame. Anyway, one bright morning Wagenson wakes up and starts to build walls around these little pockets of people. Nobody noticed for a while. I mean, if you're building a wall around ten square miles of something, it's going to take a while before anybody realizes he's having to step over something to get in, or step around something to get out.

"Pretty soon, though, people started to get a funny feeling. They started getting jittery. But not soon enough. Just when the whole thing hits 'em between the eyes, the gates go up on top and it's too late."

"But what about the newspapers?" Gar asked. "Why didn't they say something?"

"Ah, because by that time, old Wagenson already has 'em printing happy news," Frannie answered. "You know, news that's good for the country. News that supported him. That was his big bag. He wanted, and got, people in Washington who would back him up. He wanted, and got, those people to do what he wanted. The newspapers, just like television, got knocked off right away."

107

"The Constitution," said Gar, "guaranteed freedom of the press."

"Honey," Frannie said, shaking her head, "Wagenson collected all the copies of that he could find and burned them. Then he said, O.K. folks, forget that old thing. It never existed. It was never real. It doesn't take too much fear to make people forget. You're just a little too late."

"What happened next?" Tank asked. "In the homogenous communities, I mean."

"First off, Tank," Frannie went on, "we got to calling a spade a spade. A ghetto didn't just change overnight into a pretty-sounding 'homogenous community.' It was still a ghetto."

"Then what?" Gar asked impatiently.

"Well, for a while, nothing. Everybody was too scared. But one morning a fella looks over the wall and he sees that there aren't any houses on the other side. Sly old Wagenson just had 'em torn down. All around the ghettos, he tore the buildings down. When he got ready to explain things, he said it was a whole lot cheaper building the wall and tearing what was left around it down than it would be building good housing for the blacks somewhere else and moving them. I expect he was right."

"That's why the homogen—ghettos—are always so close to the cities, then, isn't it?" D.J. wondered.

"Right," said Frannie.

"You could have declared independence," Gar said. "You could have taken everything over and had your own cities and towns and maybe even countries."

"Boy, you sure are a fire-eater, aren't you?" Frannie said to him. "All the time, it's fighting with you."

Gar felt hot. He knew Frannie was right. He knew suddenly that what he hated most wasn't not being the real leader, but not being able to fight. Having to run away. It would have made Elizabeth angry, too. "It is, because it has to be," Gar said finally, a little pleased with himself.

"Well," Frannie mused, "I agree with you. I guess a lot of people agree with you. Now. That's why I ran away."

"Why?" Tank asked.

"Because I heard about the Underground," Frannie answered. "I heard there *were* people beginning to fight back. Lots of people. Old ones and young ones. All secret, but growing stronger. I thought finally something might happen that would make a difference. I just wanted to be there when it did happen. I wanted to join in."

"Terrific!" D.J. said. "So here you are, running away all over again, from the same thing, instead of standing and fighting back."

"True," Frannie smiled. "True. But when *you* have to stand and fight, at least now I'll be there, too."

She looked quickly around at the faces near her, as though afraid someone would say they didn't want her. No one did. She grinned. "I'm a big girl," Frannie said. "I'm a big target. But I'm also one hell of a bomb."

19

Huddled together for comfort and warmth the group had settled for what remained of the night and slept. At the first rays of dawn, Frannie stirred. She rarely slept as late, or as soundly, as the others. Carefully, she eased her big frame up, out and away from them.

She first scanned the countryside. They had fallen in among some bushes that grew high enough to shelter them, high enough to hide them even if they should sit up. From where she stood, Frannie could see only the bright red of Tank's sweater—she would have to do something about that—and Never Ready's feet sticking out from the underbrush.

Looking back over the route they had taken, Frannie guessed they had walked between five and six miles from the ridge, which she could see faintly in the distance. She shook her head worriedly. It wasn't far enough. They hadn't travelled fast enough. And, worst of all, the skies were clear and the sun strong. From a distance they could be seen if they moved during daylight.

Frannie idly stooped to pick a few blackberries. It was something to do, something to eat. No one had eaten, after all, last night, which was probably just as well. She guessed they had another five miles to go before trying to find Raph. And what if he had nothing to share?

Stuffing her pockets and her mouth with late berries occupied her for a while. She canvassed the area around the group, bending and stooping and pruning as she went, eating all the time. One of the little details she had left out of her story the night before was that her father had been one of the community's best cooks. She wondered if he had been a laborer of some other kind whether today she would be quite so imposing. She was used to herself now. But every so often she wondered what she would look like weighing one hundred and five, or ten. She smiled to herself. When she fell in love, then finally she would stop.

But would anyone fall in love with her the way she was? "Take me as I am or not at all," Frannie muttered to herself and turned back to the group.

She scavenged for firewood quietly. With easy expertise she laid out the wood and lit it. Freddy was the first to sit up. "Boy!" he said. "Does that feel good!"

Frannie nodded and smiled at him. He knew nothing but he was nice, she thought. She liked him. She liked his openness, his questions, his trusting.

"Do you want me to get everyone up?" he asked her.

"Not yet," she whispered. "The more sleep they get now, the less they'll need later."

"What happens now, Frannie?"

"I'm not sure," Frannie admitted. "I don't think we should move much. Hiking at night's best."

"But what will we *do*?" Freddy asked.

"I guess the best thing would be to look for things to eat."

"Around here?" Freddy asked astonished.

"Sure. You can't see from here, but there are potato fields over there. And wild rhubarb."

"Ech!" said Freddy.

"That's not the ideal meal," Frannie said, smiling at

111

him, "but maybe we can find other things, too. Like here, these berries."

Freddy's eyes opened wide at the pile of fruit Frannie had behind her. "Go ahead," Frannie urged. "We'll find more."

Freddy reached out and swallowed fistfuls without stopping. Finally he grinned at Frannie. Squatting down near her, he smiled nonstop. "I never met anyone like you," he said.

"You mean black?"

"Um-hmm. We don't have anyone like you in our town," Freddy said.

"Do I scare you?"

"Not any more. A little at first, though," Freddy said, still grinning.

"Honest little cuss," Frannie said.

"Your hands are different colors," noted Freddy.

Frannie looked at the backs of her hands and then turned them over. "Why, so they are!" she pretended. "I wonder why."

"You probably wash them too much," said Freddy seriously. "The same with your hair."

Frannie laughed.

Then she stood up. She seemed to be scenting the air. "Freddy," she said quietly, "take off your jacket."

"Why?"

"Just take it off and cover your sister with it," Frannie commanded. "Make sure we can't see any of her sweater."

"But—" Freddy started.

"Do it!"

Freddy did. Carefully he adjusted his windbreaker over the top half of Tank's body. Within seconds, not a glimpse of red wool could be seen.

112

"Good," Frannie said. "Now find a place under the bushes where you can't see the sun. So that if someone were standing up high in the sky they couldn't see you."

As Freddy ferretted in the brush, the first sounds could be heard.

In the distance, perhaps a mile north of where Frannie sat, were three Army helicopters. They flew some yards apart, moving slowly from the ridge to the river, past fields and shacks and stacks of dried hay.

Frannie narrowed her eyes to watch. The sun was still low in the sky. They must have set out at dawn.

Obviously, the people hunting these kids weren't really sure what trail to follow. But they were close enough, Frannie decided, and would get closer after a few passes turned up nothing.

Squatting beneath shrubbery, seeing that except for Freddy everyone was still sleeping, Frannie squinted into the early morning air. The helicopters were about level with her now, though still a mile north. They weren't circling, just slowly moving across the valley, sweeping trees and fields and bushes, looking for telltale signs or colors or campfires.

Campfires! Frannie threw herself on top of the small fire she had started. With both hands, she scooped up dirt and wet leaves and pebbles and anything else she could grasp. Finally, desperately, she took off her own jacket and smothered the remaining coals. Her hands could feel the heat rising and scorching the wool. But at last there was no more smoke.

Sweating, she looked up. The planes hadn't caught sight of the wispy gray trail in the early morning air. They continued on, droning into the western sky now, still only a hundred feet from the ground—but not turning her way. After a few minutes, their sound and they themselves had disappeared in the distance.

"Are you all right?" asked Freddy, crawling out from his hideaway to where Frannie was still kneeling with her hands on her burned jacket.

"For a while," Frannie said. "Better get the others up now, Freddy. We have a little talking to do."

D.J. and Gar awoke immediately. Never Ready, who was curled around Tank, was slower. He opened his eyes gradually and then shut them again. He sat up, eyes still clenched shut, and started swinging his arms in a circle around him. Tank ducked and started to laugh. Never Ready's eyes snapped open at the sound. "What's so funny?" he demanded. "It's the way I always wake up. It keeps me in shape."

"Terrific!" Frannie said. "But I think running is probably just as good for you. I hope so, anyway."

"What's happening?" D.J. asked.

"Ohhh," Tank said, "I'd love to take a bath."

"That'll have to wait, honey," Frannie said kindly. "We've got other things on our minds now."

"What?" D.J. insisted.

But Frannie didn't have to answer. "Shhh!" she cautioned.

Everyone froze. In the distance came the slight droning sound of the helicopters, on their way back. Frannie stood up and popped her head through the branches above her. The planes were making a return sweep, this time further south. They would pass right over the group.

"The Army's out looking," Frannie announced, ducking back down. "Everybody hide!"

Freddy ran back to where he'd hidden before. Gar and D.J. drove into the undergrowth, covering themselves as best they could with whatever natural foliage they found.

Frannie dug her way into a little warren. "If you can't see the open sky," she called, "they probably can't see you."

Tank stood in the center of the little covert, looking frantically around for a place to hide. The drone of the helicopters came nearer.

"Tank!" screamed Frannie. "Get down!"

But Tank seemed confused, sleepy, uncertain. There were tears of fear starting, and she seemed unable to move.

Without warning, Tank was knocked off her feet by Never Ready, who flew at her out of the bushes in which he had been crouching. His body broke her fall, and covered her red sweater completely as he lay on top of her, his hand over her mouth, his lips against her forehead.

The covert was surrounded by wind—by wind and a shattering, clattering wave of sound as one of the helicopters passed directly overhead. D.J., lying on his back, tried to look up through the leaves. He would have sworn he saw Chanler's face peering down at him from a window in the plane above, but he knew he was imagining only what he expected to see.

The planes flew past, the chattering and swirling swimming across the field and back toward the ridge from which they had started the night before. No one moved until finally Frannie announced, "O.K."

Tank let her eyes close at last, and her body relaxed beneath Never Ready's. Never Ready wasn't sure what to do. He had acted without thinking first. Should he explain why he did what he did, or would she understand? Worse,

115

he thought suddenly, feeling strangely elated as he lay atop her, would she understand what he was feeling just then, right at that very minute? He was embarrassed. Was she? Wasn't it natural? But was it natural now, here?

Shivering a little, Never Ready slid off to one side. Tank's eyes followed him. Tenderly, she reached out with one hand and stroked his hair. She smiled at him.

Never Ready felt like jumping to his feet and dancing wildly in the little circle. Instead he sat up and looked to see if the others had been watching. He couldn't see D.J. and Gar yet, though he could hear them coming out from their dens. Freddy's back was turned to him, but Frannie stood up straight, her arms akimbo, smiling at him. Never Ready blushed. Frannie winked.

Never Ready uncurled and stood up, looking in the direction the helicopters had taken, afraid to look back down at Tank. "The early bird catches the worm," he said philosophically.

"Do tell," chuckled Frannie.

"We'd better get out of here," said Gar as he stepped into the open.

"That's the problem, boy," Frannie said. "Where can we go?"

D.J. stood between them. "There must be other places like this. We'll just have to go from one to the other. They won't use helicopters all day. They'll start out on foot soon."

"Great!" Never Ready said.

"Well," answered Frannie, "we know the countryside about as well as they do. It's a better match than us against their planes."

Tank leaned on an elbow. "Maybe we could find a river

116

or something. There would be bushes and things on the banks and we could hide if we had to."

"I think we'd better forget about smelling sweet for a while," D.J. said a little harshly. "Frannie," he went on, "where are we?"

"Nowhere, baby," she replied. "In the middle of nowhere."

"I mean, how far are we from Altoona, or your friend's place?"

"Raph?" Frannie asked. "He hasn't exactly got a place. He just sort of runs a territory. We're about five miles away, I'd guess."

"I'm hungry," Freddy announced.

Never Ready knelt and looked earnestly at Freddy. "You can't have your cake and eat it, too," he advised.

"But I haven't got any cake," Freddy complained.

"What I mean, Freddy," Never Ready explained, "is that not being caught is more important than food. We all have to wait."

"All right," Frannie announced. "Let's go."

"Where?" D.J. asked.

"Never you mind," she answered. "You just pull yourself together and follow me."

Gar stooped and looked at both food parcels. Then he started to dig into the ground with his heel. He buried the wicker basket after transferring what had been left in it into the canvas carryall. The others stood around watching and waiting for him to finish.

"O.K.," he said finally. "Let's go."

"Before we do," Frannie said, "I'd like to ask one little question."

"What?" D.J. asked.

"You said you were on your way to Altoona. When you get there, if we get there, and if you really do get this other kid—"

"Robin," Freddy interjected.

"Right," Frannie went on. "If you really do bust this kid out, then where do you go? Is someone waiting for you somewhere? Where is it you're finally going to be safe?"

No one answered. Tank looked down at her shoes and scuffed them softly. Never Ready looked at Gar, expecting him to answer. But Gar couldn't, not honestly. D.J. just stood facing the sun.

"Terrific!" snorted Frannie.

20

For the next few hours, the six ducked and dropped, searched and sprinted across the open country. One by one they moved from cover to cover. First Frannie, then Tank and Freddy, Gar, Never Ready, and finally D.J. As soon as all six stood again together, Frannie would take off once more.

They were heading north now, a little out of their way. Frannie convinced them that since the copters had already passed over this territory, they weren't likely to do so again. At least, not right away. She had a destination in mind that she would disclose to no one, not even D.J. Everybody would just have to trust her.

For Frannie had been running and hiding, scavenging and sleeping in the open for a much longer time than they had. She knew which berries could be nibbled, which would probably give them cramps. She knew which water could be drunk without fear. She had a keen sense of direction and an unerring sense of grace as she dove and dodged across the fields. It began to seem as though she had lived and survived in the open all her life.

At noon, Frannie called a stop in a small grove of trees. "If we're lucky," she said when everyone had caught up to her, "we'll be eating hot food tonight. So you may as well polish off whatever's left now."

Gar opened the canvas bag and showed its contents around. One can of cream of asparagus soup and one

119

large chocolate bar. D.J. opened the can while Tank broke the chocolate into six pieces.

"Not for me, thanks," Frannie said when Tank tried to get her to take a piece of chocolate. "I've got so much fat on me now I could run for days and not get hungry."

Tank gave the extra piece to Freddy.

Before they started out again, Gar climbed the tallest of the trees in the stand and surveyed the ground they had covered.

"See anything?" D.J. called up at him.

"No," Gar answered. "Not yet."

"Count your blessings instead of sheep," Never Ready said aloud.

"What?" asked Freddy.

"Never mind," Never Ready said. "It's just something I say a lot."

"Wait a minute!" shouted Gar, still atop the tallest pine. "Wait a minute."

The five people below him stood stock still.

"What is it?" D.J. whispered up into the branches.

"A copter," Gar answered. "No, two of them."

"Where?" Frannie asked.

"I can't be sure," Gar said. "It looks like they're about where we were this morning."

"Terrific," Frannie muttered, putting her foot on the lowest branch of Gar's tree. Before anyone could ask what she was doing, Frannie was half way up the trunk of the tree, delicately stretching out as she reached the same limb on which Gar sat.

No one asked Frannie what she saw. She would tell them herself when she was ready.

Shading her eyes, Frannie squinted into the distance. Yes, there were two copters, but just hovering, not skimming. She stared at them. Actually, they *were* moving but ever so slowly, as though following someone along the ground.

"Oh, my God!" Frannie gasped. She slid down through the branches. Gar was right behind her.

"What is it?" D.J. asked urgently.

"I'm not sure," Frannie said. "I'm only guessing."

"What?" Gar asked as he hit the ground.

"It looks to me," Frannie began slowly, "like they're following something. And I'll bet my cousin's diploma that what they're following is dogs."

"Dogs?" Freddy asked.

"Bloodhounds," Frannie explained.

"Jesus!" Gar said. No one else said anything.

"Don't ask me what we do now," Frannie said, sinking down onto the ground and folding her legs under her. "What I'd like is to sit here and wait for them to come get me. I'm tired."

"This is no time to give up," D.J. said.

"Take over, chief," Frannie said to him. "I just haven't got it in me."

"You have to," Gar said firmly.

"If at first you don't succeed, try, try again," Never Ready counselled.

"The river!" Gar said. "There's a river about half a mile from here. I saw it from up there."

"That's no good," said Frannie. "They'll track us right into the water."

"Well, give up if you want to," Gar announced angrily, "but I'm getting out of here."

"We're with you," Never Ready said, grabbing Tank's good arm and hauling her to her feet.

"D.J.?" asked Gar.

121

"Right," D.J. said. "Frannie, we followed you all this time. We trusted you."

"So?" said Frannie.

"You have to trust us now," D.J. said to her.

Frannie looked up at D.J. and then grinned. "Boy," she said, "when you get earnest, you're just plain irresistible!" She heaved herself to her feet and shook herself out.

Gar took the lead this time. He didn't stop to crouch or hide. He ran straight forward, toward the water he had seen glistening under the trees in the distance, across a dirt road that ran alongside the stream. Caution wasn't what was needed now, he knew; speed was.

Soon they stood on the rocky ledge that followed the water's progress. Breathing deeply, everyone stared at the stream's course and current, which were slow, and at its bed which was shallow and shale-filled.

"I wonder if it's cold," said Tank, bending down to put a hand in. She looked happily back up at the others. "It's nice. The sun warms it."

"How fast you figure they can go?" D.J. asked Frannie.

"Not so fast as we just did," Frannie said.

"They're a couple of hours behind, maybe?" D.J. asked again.

"Depends," said Frannie, "on how fast those dogs get the scent. How fast their trainers can follow, too, I guess."

"All right. Now, everybody listen," D.J. said. "Don't ask questions. Just listen and then do as I say."

All eyes looked expectantly at D.J.

"I want everyone to fan out—south, not north of here —and stay on this side of the river. Pick up whatever paper and tin cans and metal you can find. Then bring it all back here to me."

"Why?" Freddy asked.

122

"Freddy," D.J. said warningly, "just do it."

D.J. stood at the water's edge as the others moved along the river bank. He saw them bending down, picking up the things he had ordered. They worked fast and well, without knowing why.

Within ten minutes, all stood again in a circle. At their feet were discarded soda and beer cans, old and rotting newspapers, a few flat pieces of scrap metal.

"Now what?" asked Frannie.

"Here's your chance, Gar," D.J. said, "to get a *little* exercise in. Flatten every can you can, as fast as you can."

"Now?" asked Gar.

"Now."

Gar bent down and picked up the first can. Without straining, he put the can between the palms of his hands and squeezed. In seconds the metal was reshaped into a flat surface. He handed it to D.J. and bent down to get another.

Never Ready watched. Then he too bent down and took a can. Straightening up, he placed the metal between his hands and squeezed mightily and fast. "Damn!" he said. "You might know." What he had done was crack the can in the middle and push it into a roundish, glitteringly unusable shape.

"Don't try," D.J. said. "Let Gar do it. We can't afford to waste them."

Gar flattened nearly twenty cans. "That's enough," D.J. said. "You can stop."

"I get it!" Frannie said suddenly. She stooped down and picked up a few heavy pieces of the scrap metal and held them a moment. She turned around and threw first one and then another piece of metal out a few feet ahead. "Watch," she said to them all.

123

Frannie hopped from where she was standing, and landed on the first piece of metal. Precariously swaying on one foot for a moment, she got her balance and then stretched out her other leg toward the second piece. She jumped a little and then stood steadily on the second metal stone.

She turned around and smiled at D.J. "Right?" she asked.

"Absolutely," D.J. said. "You see," he said to the others, "metal and paper don't hold smells. And if they do, they won't hold them very long. The dogs won't be able to track us any farther than here if we use these."

"But D.J.," Gar said, "we can't move very fast this way."

"We'll lose our lead," Never Ready added.

"No, we won't," D.J. said firmly. "First of all, when they do pick up our scent and get here, they'll think we crossed the river. The water will stop the dogs a minute, but the men will know what to do. They'll hit the other side and expect to find tracks or smells there. But there won't be any."

"For someone who just started playing this game," Frannie said admiringly, "you do some mighty heavy thinking."

D.J. smiled. "It'll be slow," he said, "but if we can do it for maybe a mile, I think we'll be all right."

Gar looked into the pile of metal and scrap at his feet. "I count thirty good pieces," he said.

Never Ready counted. "We need ten to stand on, and twenty to move with."

"One by one?" Tank asked.

"Like a train!" Freddy said happily.

"Won't they see the marks?" Gar asked. "The cans will

124

sink into the ground a little when we step on them."

"That's a chance we have to take," D.J. said.

Gar bent down and grabbed half a dozen squashed cans. "Which way, D.J.?" he asked.

"North," D.J. answered, pointing. "On this side of the water. We'll cross later."

Gar turned north and stood still a moment. Then he tossed two cans in front of himself. He jumped from where he stood onto the first easily, and then leapt from there to the second one. He bent again and threw two more pieces of metal ahead. When he had jumped and jiggled his way across the six cans he had started with, he turned and looked behind himself.

Frannie was jumping along the same path with a handful of metal in her arms. When she got to where Gar stood she handed him what she was carrying and then watched as he threw them out ahead. He jumped again and she followed. When they had gone a few more paces, they stopped and waited.

Never Ready came next, jumping from the cans they had already strewn along the path to where he caught up with them. He handed some more metal to Frannie who passed it to Gar. Gar threw it forward.

Tank followed, carrying more, and then D.J. picked up Freddy piggy-back style and started out. But as D.J. left each can and landed on the next, he had to bend down and pick up the metal from behind him. By the time he and Freddy reached the others, D.J. was winded but he carried twenty pieces of metal with him.

He reached out to Tank who took the pile from him and passed it to Never Ready, Frannie and finally to Gar. Then D.J. gave Tank some dry pieces of paper to pass forward as well, paper he had collected and stuck in his

125

belt as he started out. Together, with the cans, they could reach nearly forty paces before having to stop.

It was long hot work. D.J. passed Freddy along to Never Ready who jumped with Freddy aboard for a while. Then Freddy was handed to Frannie who was strong enough to help. Finally Freddy landed on Gar's back.

Frannie stood motionless on paper and can. "Listen," she said.

A dull, constant sound came at them through the trees: helicopters. Under this, a distant baying could be heard as well.

"I'd guess they're still maybe a mile behind," Frannie said. "If we're going to cross, we'd better get cracking."

D.J. nodded. He was leading the group now, beginning to toss the pieces of paper and metal in a gentle arc toward the river. Within minutes he stood at its bank, the others ranging behind him, holding their stepping-stones.

"We'll have to cross with all of these," D.J. said, pointing at the bunch of metal slivers in Tank's hands. "We don't want them left behind and found."

Everyone understood. Gar passed Freddy across to D.J. Settling Freddy as comfortably as possible on his back, D.J. bent down and slid a flattened can into the water before him. The can glittered as it cut sideways through the stream and settled on the bottom. D.J. smiled. The river would cover the small depressions the cans would make.

He turned around and pointed to what he had done. Then he began to cross.

The portage went without mishap, except that Frannie had to whisper at Tank sharply to hurry up. Tank had gotten half way across the river and had stopped, stooping down to dip her hands and face in the rushing stream.

Gar was the last to cross, and he brought with him the remaining cans. "We'd better use them a while more," he said to D.J. "If they do look for us on this side, they'll look for footprints in the mud."

Again the painstaking progress began, now away from the river and toward the covering underbrush that accompanied the river's course.

After four turns with the stepstones, D.J. decided they could stop. Again Gar began digging in the soft earth with his heel, and when the hole was deep and broad enough, he laid all the cans and paper and scrap metal into it. Everyone helped cover the fresh digging.

They headed west again, with Frannie leading. She was taking them toward her secret destination. She smiled and rubbed her stomach when one or the other asked her questions about her course.

West a while, and then the group began curving back, dropping south again, and west. They sneaked past collective farms, across country roads, around the outskirts of a sleepy village set deep in a cornfield. In the distance they could see another ridge of hills, higher than any they had crossed so far. From there, Frannie said, they could see the prison at Altoona—if the night was clear.

They could no longer hear the hounds behind them. No helicopters swept above. They began to feel safe in their flight, confident of their pilot.

As the afternoon light began to fade, Frannie called a halt. "But why here?" D.J. asked. "We don't seem to be anywhere."

"You don't know how close we are," said Frannie with a wide grin. "You're in for a surprise."

127

21

Frannie made them all rest, whether or not they wanted to sleep. Within a few hours, darkness fell around them as though it was hurrying to help. D.J. checked his wristwatch; at eight o'clock they had been stationary for more than three hours. He wondered how much longer they would have to wait. Even he, now, was hungry. He looked at Freddy, asleep in Tank's lap. That was a good thing, anyway.

At nine o'clock Frannie roused everyone. Urging them not to talk and to follow her, she slowly began wending through birch and sumac and over fallen trees until she stood at the edge of a planted field. Even in the faint light of the moon, they could see the furrows.

Without warning, Frannie ducked and ran directly across the field, following the seeded rows. Trusting, everyone else followed, well spaced and with caution. They gathered around her and waited.

"I ain't talkin' while the flavor lasts," she teased, and ducked again through some skimpy trees. She led them another three hundred yards and then ordered a halt. She pointed.

What they saw was a whitewashed building, only one story high, long and lone and single on the edge of a worked-out area. There were no lights inside. One bulb shimmered above a doorway.

"What is it?" Tank asked.

128

"The best restaurant in forty miles, honey," Frannie replied. "Only no one who eats there realizes it."

"I know what it is," Gar announced. "It's a communal kitchen. Where workers eat."

"Is there food inside?" asked D.J.

"There sure is," Frannie answered. "But don't start eating everything you can lay your hands on. There's a way of doing this—stealing, I mean—so that they hardly ever find out anything's missing."

Shh-ing everyone. Frannie beckoned them to follow her. She led them to the building's porch and together they huddled outside the front door. It was padlocked. "Oh no!" Never Ready moaned. "Now what?"

But Gar had decided what to do. He looked at the lock. It was shiny and new; it wouldn't give easily. The metal bar, though, that was attached to the frame of the building and through which the padlock hung, was old and rusty. The wood it was screwed into looked maggoty. *Maybe-maybe,* thought Gar.

He put both hands as close together on the crossbar as he could. He took two deep breaths and then, with all his strength, Gar yanked downwards on the bar. The padlock held. The screws did not. Beaming, Gar opened the door toward himself and stood aside, bowing them to enter.

"No lights!" warned Frannie.

Motionless, the six sensed rather than saw a long, broad room, with tables and benches throughout. In the dark, it was impossible to know where the kitchen, and supplies, might be.

A match blazed. Tank held a candle triumphantly out toward the others.

When they got to the kitchen, Frannie collected them

129

and spoke warningly again. "Now," she said, "there's a right way and a wrong way to steal. First off, we take nothing that isn't in a box or a container we can seal up again. Like pancake mix. If we want to make pancakes, we use water, not milk, and no butter. Maybe a little syrup. But we never use a whole box of anything. We take what we need and then, ever so carefully, we push the bottom of the box up again. When someone looks at it, he'll never realize it's false."

"No wonder you've picked up a little weight," D.J. said sweetly, "if all you've been into is pancakes."

Frannie ignored D.J. "Now, let's see what's what," she said.

What was what was pancake mix, cake mix, flour. Miraculously, Gar found some Scotch tape, which meant that they could patch up containers of milk and ground beef. There were cans of soup that could be tampered with, lining them with waxed paper and taping their bottoms back on. There was even ice cream in containers that could be fixed up again.

The kitchen was lit by two candles only. They had covered the windows of the shed with their jackets. An air of happiness and adventure was nearly visible as they discovered and planned and cooked and ate. They looked up at the big television set above the stove and wondered if they dare turn it on, just for fun.

Tank disappeared as soon as she could and went into the ladies' washroom. They could hear the water from the tap there pouring out endlessly. Little wisps of steam came slithering under the door.

"Can we sleep here tonight?" Freddy asked Frannie.

Frannie turned to D.J. for an answer. "I don't see why not," he said. "The only thing is, what time do people start arriving in the morning?"

"About five," Frannie said. "We could each take turns staying up, just in case."

"I'll tell you what," Never Ready volunteered, "why don't D.J. and Gar and I keep watch, and all of you can get a full night's sleep. Tomorrow you and Tank can stand guard."

"Oh," said Tank, wandering sleepily back into the room, "that would be wonderful."

The issue was decided. Everyone found a comfortable spot. The hard floors and sharp corners they curled around seemed almost soft after the previous night spent among pine needles, pine cones, grass, weeds and trash. At least here there was a roof over their heads; at least here, when they awoke in the morning, they wouldn't be wet and shivering from early morning dew.

Never Ready was first to stand watch. It was just past ten o'clock. He would stay awake for two hours and then wake either Gar or D.J., who would stand watch for another two hours. At four everyone would arise and take to the trail.

Never Ready watched as the others got comfortable. He looked protectively at Tank as she made a pillow of her sweater and lay down not far from the oven. It had been left on, low, so that the room would stay warm and dry.

Never Ready leaned back against the wall. He was not displeased with things so far. He thought briefly about Elizabeth. There hadn't been time really to think about her, or even about his own family. He was a little ashamed when he remembered what so far he had had time to think about.

"My fellow Americans."

131

Freddy screamed. Frannie jumped to her feet and looked around, ready to run or pounce. Gar was already on his feet, a kitchen knife in hand.

"It is with a heavy heart that I address you tonight."

The picture above the stove finally cleared and the light came up full. The set had been turned on automatically, pre-empting not only all other channels, but activating even the sets across the country that were turned off. The sound had begun before the picture was fully in view.

"You will recall," said the speaker, "that it was nearly twelve years ago when I first asked you to support me and my administration. I asked, and you granted my request. We needed your support to put this country back on the right tracks again, the tracks that led toward honor and peace abroad and at home."

D.J. watched the man on the screen. He had forgotten how much Wagenson and his father looked alike. They were about the same age. They were both dark. They always seemed to need a shave. Wagenson's features, though, were firmer than D.J.'s father's. There was the famous straight, almost too perfect nose; the high cheekbones that people always said showed that Wagenson came from good stock. But the eyes were the same: shifty, fast-moving, never-resting little ball-bearings under heavy brows. Unless Wagenson was addressing the country; then he looked straight into the camera with a look that passed for real sincerity and concern.

"I asked you to send to Washington men who would support, not fight, the President's plans and promises. I told you that with this kind of support, we could stop crime in the streets, stop social injustices, start at last to end a foreign war with a negotiated settlement."

132

The camera pulled back. Gar gasped. It was more than just a routine speech. For there were the Joint Chiefs of Staff, the Senate President, the House Speaker, and there —for the first time in years—was Mitchell, sitting hunched in a chair next to Wagenson, looking a hundred years old. Of course, Gar recalled, the Attorney General probably wasn't much more than seventy-five. But he had been around so long, longer even than Wagenson, that people naturally assumed he had been present at the founding of the Republic.

Gar concentrated. This was the first time anyone had seen Mitchell since Hoover had died. Mitchell had taken over the F.B.I. then, added it to his Justice Department and to his crowd at Internal Security. He was a man mostly legend, all fear.

"You know," Wagenson continued, "how many and how well we have kept our pledges. To be sure, we have had to go without some things for the nation's good. We have had at times to suspend certain rights and privileges of some of our citizens in order to better protect not only them but all of us. We have had to censor, from time to time, matters of national security from our press and magazines and networks. We have had to destroy whole mountains of obscenity, novels of smut and pornography, books critical of this country and her greatness."

Frannie relaxed. This was beginning to sound like another ordinary call to arms. The enemy within, she thought to herself. She remembered reading in one of the "obscene" books how Russia, during its early years of communism, had had to keep alerting its people to the danger from without, the danger massed on her borders. And each warning had almost always been followed by a purge of one kind or another, in which people who did this or that, said this or that, were arrested or executed or informed upon by their neighbors. She relaxed, because she couldn't possibly imagine what group had not already been purged and relocated.

Who else was there, Frannie asked herself, to corral, to imprison and torture and expel from society? The blacks were gone. The Indians and Chinese and native Japanese were gone. There had been some talk of starting homogenous communities for Italians and Jews. Since she had heard nothing more, Frannie assumed those ideas had been set aside as impractical. The handicapped had places of their own. The pre-criminal kids just kept being tested and encamped. And the opposition—well, as far as Frannie knew, there hadn't been any real political opposition in years.

"The country has been, for some time now, quiet and safe and healthy economically," the President went on. "Our internal problems have gradually been solving themselves. I told you when first I took office that there *are* simple answers to some of the most important questions we face. There are now and there were then.

"But now, suddenly, without reason or warning, the enemy has shown its long-maned head again. Citizens in all parts of this great nation have been kidnapped. Responsible members of society have disappeared, leaving their families and friends and co-workers puzzled and sad. There is once again a massive conspiracy here on our own shores. A conspiracy we must, if we are to survive as a nation of greatness, stamp out."

"Hooo!" shouted D.J. "Gar, that must mean the Underground really is going at it!"

Gar nodded. "He sounds scared, doesn't he?"

"Sure," D.J. said. "His Special Forces are being picked

134

off, one by one. How can he keep everyone terrified and under control without them?"

"Now," Wagenson said, "our government has not been standing idly by while these revolutionaries have tried to destroy our citizenry. My colleague, the Attorney General, and his brave and well-trained staffs, have been working round the clock, at my own explicit order, to begin apprehending these disrupters of our American way of life.

"Mr. Mitchell will describe in more detail some of the people the government now seeks as traitors and revolutionaries. After he has spoken, the governors of each of your sovereign states will take to the air to tell you particularly, in each locale, what you can do to help us in this new and dangerous fight.

"But let me make one thing perfectly clear: even though these revolutionaries are well trained and determined to embarrass us at home and abroad, I give you my word, my fellow Americans, that with your support this administration will be able, once again, to provide a country that is safe and healthy, whose economy is sound, whose ideals are honored throughout the world. A new nation can be forged from our efforts tonight. A new nation that need never know civil strife or fear. We may ask you for sacrifices, some even greater and perhaps more saddening than those we have had to ask for in the past. But when this present danger is past, the country will once again be the country *you* want, the country our forefathers envisioned. And in which we may finally, at last, come to have what we have all dreamed about for decades: a full generation of peace for our children. Thank you, and good night."

"What does all that mean?" Tank asked.

135

"Never mind, honey," Frannie said softly. "It's nothing to worry about."

"I want to speak briefly to you out there, my friends," began Mitchell in a voice crusty with age, "and I do mean briefly. I've always liked to think I was a weak public speaker and rather a stronger public servant."

The Attorney General tried to smile. His face could only break into creases.

"You have heard the President. We need your help. We're not offering rewards or plaques, pledges or promises, for what we ask. We're only requesting that each and every one of you do your duty as citizens of this great nation. If you want, as we certainly do, to stop a new reign of terror in the streets, we will need your help.

"Please simply call your local law enforcement agency at the first suspicion you may have of your acquaintances, your friends, even your family members. It is our feeling that all of us may be surprised at the depth and breadth of this new conspiracy. We're not asking honorable men to become informers. We are suggesting that each state, as the sovereign state of Indiana did years ago, empower its citizens to act on information gathered about crime themselves, as representatives of the law-abiding community. We will slowly and with great care and purpose investigate all leads we get from you. There will be no sudden, hysterical action. What we want is justice and order, justice and peace.

"Our great country has always responded immediately and well in times of crisis. This is one of those times. I know you won't fail us.

"Now, in each five-state area, the governors of your own states have taped this afternoon an address, a list of people we already know to be dangerous and who are at

136

large. Those of you in California, for example, will hear not only from your own governor, but from the governors of Oregon, Nevada, Utah, and Arizona. Listen carefully. Think back. Remember.

"We can only help you if you help us. Remember that, too. Good night."

"Christ!" D.J. exploded. "It's not enough he's got spies in every town in the whole country. Now he wants spies to spy on spies!"

There was a flickering on the screen. The six sat upright and motionless, holding their breaths, knowing that now, if ever they needed help as they fled they could expect to get it only by threats and fear. Never from honest sympathy. It was as though Chanler had used the President's appearance to say, *"En garde!"*

"Who's that?" Tank asked, looking at a man in his middle fifties with a full head of curly white hair.

"That," said Frannie, "is the esteemed Governor of Nebraska, where my own sweet little ghetto was. Where it still is and where, I'm happy to say, I ain't."

"Ladies and gentlemen," began the Governor of Nebraska, "please listen carefully and make notes if you wish. This is only the first such broadcast I will make. From now until the time this insurrection is quelled, I will address you with the same kind of information each evening, a little earlier than now, at nine o'clock.

"Among the people the State of Nebraska is searching for are the following," and he began to read. He started with the A's and continued rapidly on to the B's. Frannie fidgeted. "Will he call your name?" asked Tank.

"Probably," Frannie said. "I've been on the road a long time."

The governor didn't take long to reach the H's. And

137

then, when it did happen, it happened so fast it seemed as though it was something dreamed, not real.

"Frances Eleanor Heffernan, fifteen. Black, one hundred and sixty pounds. Considered dangerous. May be armed. Thought to be fleeing alone. Wanted for theft, arson, inciting a riot."

"What!" Frannie shouted, jumping to her feet. "What the fuck is that about?"

"Easy, Frannie," said D.J., standing up and coming to her.

"You don't believe that, do you?" asked Frannie frantically. "I mean, that's just plain lying!"

"Of course we don't believe it," D.J. said, trying to calm her. "They've just used you as a scapegoat, an easy target, someone to blame everything that's been going wrong on."

"But Jesus," Frannie said, "suppose someone really does believe it. Why, I'd be shot on sight!"

"Shhh!" Never Ready said as the screen flickered and another man's face was seen. "It's our turn."

The Governor of Iowa began reading his list. What he read about each of the people who had gathered together one night to flee Chanler was simple and direct.

"Garfield Bennett, fourteen. Medium height, very strong build. Wanted for inciting to riot and obstructing justice."

"Daniel J. Berryman, Jr., sixteen. Six feet one inch tall, dark hair. Wanted for obstructing justice, sabotage, inciting to riot."

"Anthony John Newman, the Third, also known as 'Never Ready,' aged fourteen. Medium height and build, black hair. Wanted for obstructing justice, kidnapping, inciting to riot."

"Why'd he pick me?" Never Ready wondered. "I didn't kidnap anyone alone."

"Shhh!" Gar said, still listening.

The Governor continued reading. "Frederick McDonald Wheeler, nine. Thin, about five feet tall, handicapped, may be walking with a limp. Wanted for evading health authorities, inciting to riot."

"What does that mean, that last?" asked Freddy.

"Nothing important," D.J. said.

"I wonder if I did it," Freddy grinned. "Maybe it would be fun."

"Julia King Wheeler, thirteen. Five feet five, one hundred and thirty-odd pounds. Thought to be injured and may be dangerous. Wanted for inciting to riot, obstruction of justice."

"Hey, Gar!" Never Ready said. "He didn't mention Elizabeth."

"He doesn't have to," Gar said. "They've already got her. What bothers me is that he didn't say anything about my parents."

Everyone fell silent.

"That doesn't mean," D.J. said, "that they've been taken."

Frannie sat down. "Well," she said, "it doesn't do any good to worry about things tonight. We'll need our strength tomorrow."

She hugged her knees and rolled over onto the floor, trying to make herself relax. But her eyes stayed open.

The others waited until the reading from the screen was finished. Then they, too, tried again to sleep. Except for Never Ready, who was still the first guard.

D.J. lay down. He looked at Gar, lying on his back, looking at the ceiling and the pipes above. He wished he

139

could say something to Gar that would put his mind at rest, that would make a difference, that would help. But there was nothing. Elizabeth was gone. Gar's parents might have been taken. It was all terrible to think about.

D.J. stared at the ceiling, too. He tried to imagine what detention prisons were like. He remembered Robin Frye. If it weren't for him, D.J. thought, by now they might all be safe somewhere instead of on the run. Then D.J. remembered something else: were it not for him, D.J. himself, Robin Frye would still be free.

And what about his own father? D.J. was almost certain his father was in prison, too. There wasn't much the authorities could get from him. He knew nothing of the plan to kidnap Chanler, nothing of their escape through town and across the countryside.

D.J. wanted to feel a little sorry for his father now. But he couldn't. More and more frequently, all D.J. felt was scorn. And anger.

Sensibly, D.J. stopped thinking about his father. He would get no sleep at all if he allowed himself to get really mad, the way he wanted to, mad enough to strike out, to do something to his father the way his father had done to hundreds of other people. *Tomorrow, after I sleep,* D.J. decided, *I can hate him if I want.*

22

"**Sort of romantic,** isn't it?" Never Ready said, holding his pole out over the water and hoping no fish would be beneath it to bite.

"Do you ever dream, Anthony?" Tank asked. "I mean, with your eyes open. Daydream?"

Never Ready blushed. "Sometimes," he admitted.

"What about?" Tank wanted to know.

Never Ready coughed. "Lots of things," he said. "I mean, there are a lot of things . . . like sex."

"Sex?"

"Sure," Never Ready said more loudly, now that he had said the word and it hadn't caused the day to cloud, the sky to part. "Don't you ever think about it?"

"No," Tank said wonderingly. "I guess, in a way, I do. But what I dream about is love."

"Oh."

The new day was one of nature's gentle moments, an attempt at proving Indian Summers were neither old-fashioned nor impossible, even now. The haze that covered the countryside, that lay thick above damp fields and rose in silent trains from the streams, lifted slowly and carefully, as though someone were gently pulling back the sheets and blankets on a very large, very green bed.

Gar had everyone awake and ready to leave by four. He propped the metal bar and the lock back in place on the door frame so that at first it would look as though

141

nothing had happened to them. It was a small deception, but it made them all feel better.

They had started out, feeling their way through early morning darkness and shadow, forming into the line that would not be broken until midday. Frannie led again, taking them all toward wherever that fellow Raph was supposed to be. D.J. followed behind her, sometimes walking in step with her to talk; sometimes following a pace behind so that when Frannie wanted to speak she had to slow down and turn half around.

Freddy, Tank, and Never Ready had travelled as a trio. Tank and Never Ready flirted over Freddy's head, giggling together about little jokes they either saw or made up. Freddy hiked along as best he could, conscious of the fact that he must neither slow the group nor be a burden. Only once in a great while would he turn toward his sister and without words tell her how tired he was, how great the strain was. Tank understood and smiled encouragement. From time to time she and Never Ready put their hands under Freddy's shoulders and hoisted him aloft for a step or two. Freddy smiled at this, even laughed a little.

Gar followed them all, occasionally looking behind or stopping to listen for motors or dogs or cars. Mentally he was preparing for action. He wasn't certain how he expected to rescue that kid Frye, but he wanted to do it quickly and get on. He was anxious to turn around and start back for Elizabeth. In the morning's haze, Gar felt certain his parents, too, would need help. And then a thought came sharp and clear at him: his father, if he really had been caught, would be in Altoona. And his mother would be with Elizabeth. Oddly, he felt comforted.

142

Frannie led the group toward the high ridge they had seen the day before. Higher than the one from which they had run in darkness two days before, more rugged, better for hiding.

At noon, they had stopped near a small freshwater pond. Never Ready fashioned a fishing pole and a hook from a safety pin and sat down at its edge, singing softly to himself an old and proscribed tune, "Ol' Man River." He liked the way the song flowed, and his voice was deepening enough to sing it with feeling and full range.

Tank had wandered down to the water's edge, and had at first ignored Never Ready, throwing pebbles into the water with seeming nonchalance. But within a few minutes, she had stepped to Never Ready's side and sat down next to him, at first pretending that when she touched him it was by accident. She was happy to be resting, and the sun pleased her. Soon she had simply leaned against Never Ready and shut her eyes, her face turned toward the sun.

"I guess, though," Tank said dreamily, "that sex is part of love so we're probably thinking about the same things."

Never Ready was grateful Tank's eyes were closed so that she couldn't see and tell that while they might be thinking the same general thing, Never Ready's emphasis was a little different from Tank's.

"Everyone likes you, you know?" Tank went on. "I wonder why they do."

"What do you mean, why?" Never Ready asked, a little put out.

"Well," Tank said, sitting up and opening her eyes, "it's not that you're not nice. Or polite. Or anything. It's just something about you, I guess, that people like."

143

Never Ready smiled. "My mother says it's my fat Irish mug."

Tank examined Never Ready's face. "It's not fat," she said. And it wasn't: Never Ready had lost his baby fat years ago and his face was going to be one that was lined but appealingly so as he grew older. He had gray eyes, and they were never bloodshot, no matter how late he stayed awake or how little sleep he got. His black hair had just a little curl in it, and it was rather long around his ears, making his head seem to be placed between a wispy set of black wings and ready for flight at any moment.

"Do you want everyone to like you?" Tank asked seriously. "I mean, is that what you want most to be: President of the class?"

"I don't know," Never Ready said truthfully. "That's my biggest problem."

"What is?"

"That I don't know," Never Ready said. "Not just about that. I don't know what I want to do, or where I should live, or what I want to be like, or anything. I'm sort of in between everything right now, I guess. It makes me nervous. I'd like to be definitely someone, doing some one thing somewhere. But I don't know any of that."

"Well," Tank leaned back again, dreamily, "you've got plenty of time to make up your mind."

"But that's just it, Julie, I haven't!" Never Ready answered positively. "The one thing I do know is that I haven't got plenty of time. I mean I know people who want to be doctors, and they've always wanted to be doctors, and they go to school and take the right courses and go on to become doctors. They've got it all planned.

144

That's the way I want to be, too." He paused. "If only it were that simple."

"Well anyway," Tank said, "everyone likes you. That should make you happy."

Never Ready was a little disappointed. Here he was, sitting in the wide open, clear air with Tank, the girl he had imagined with him for months now, and she couldn't pay enough attention to what he was saying even to pretend to be interested. He *was* uncertain, and he hated it. He had never told anyone before, but now he had, and Tank just went ahead and said 'well anyway' and closed her eyes.

Being happy-go-lucky, everyone's favorite, wasn't easy. Never Ready wanted to say that, too. It meant you had to be too many different things to too many different people. You never had a chance to be yourself. Worse, you never had a chance to find out who you really were, or what. Never Ready thought of himself now as neither boy nor man. Neither as strong as Gar, nor as adventurous as D.J. Not as smart as Elizabeth, or as basic as Frannie. He wanted to be a man, and he wanted to be one soon. But, inside, he wondered if he were ready. He was ready for sex, maybe, but even with that he wasn't certain that that counted most. In fact, he knew it didn't. It might seem to for a while, but soon after he would be left with the same questions, and the same doubts, and the same cloudy picture of who he was. That was how he pictured himself—as a cloud that could be shaped into almost anything by anyone. He should do the shaping, he knew. But how? And when?

Never Ready turned his head slightly and looked down at Tank, whose head rested lightly on his shoulder. He wondered what Tank was dreaming about now. He wondered if she really did like him. She had touched him yesterday. She had let him touch her. But how did she really feel? Maybe she didn't feel anything. Maybe she just dreamed that she felt and that was supposed to be enough.

Never Ready looked at the end of his fishing pole. It hadn't wavered once since he'd been sitting there. If there were any fish in the pond, they weren't interested in being caught by the President of Their Class. Not today, anyway.

He looked again at Tank. She was smiling now, her eyes still closed. She *was* going to be beautiful. Never Ready had been right; he could tell. She was going to be so beautiful and so—maybe she was waiting for him, right now, maybe she was waiting for him to—.

He didn't know exactly what to do first. He put his fishing pole at his side, careful to balance it so that if anything should take his hook the pole wouldn't shoot into the water and disappear. He didn't want to move his shoulder. He didn't want to startle Tank. He wanted to be gentle, to be kind, to touch her ever so softly.

His right hand rose shakily and crossed his body, moving in a nervous circle toward Tank. Never Ready breathed deeply as his hand reached Tank's face. With just his fingertips, he stroked her cheek. She smiled still. "Mmmm," she said.

Never Ready touched her face again. Then he let his hand slide down to her neck. His fingers seemed to him to be someone else's as he watched them slip under her blouse collar and stroke her shoulder.

Tank sighed. She snuggled closer to Never Ready and put her hand on his thigh.

Oh God! thought Never Ready. *Don't let her hand*

146

move. Don't let it come up any farther. Oh please!

By themselves, it seemed, his fingers undid the top buttons of Tank's blouse. Never Ready could feel the silk of her slip. He stopped breathing.

It was soft. It was so soft. It was just like the slip, it was so soft.

His hand stopped moving, seeming to decide that it was now where it wanted to be and didn't want to move at all, ever.

Never Ready sighed. "Julie," he whispered.

"Is it beautiful?" Tank asked softly, her eyes still closed and her smile never wavering. "Is it really beautiful?"

"Oh, Julie!" Never Ready said again, not knowing what else in the entire world to say.

The handle of the pole next to Never Ready began to swing out from his side, tumbling across the pebbles on which it had lain. It bumped Never Ready's knee as its tip nosed into the water.

"Oh no!" Never Ready said under his breath. Wanting to move quickly to catch it, wanting to keep his hand where it was, wanting if he had to to withdraw it gently, Never Ready closed his eyes.

"I'm sorry . . . I . . . it's the fishing pole—" he managed to say.

He sat up straight and reached out for the pole in time. He grabbed it tightly and, without thinking, jerked it out of the water.

There was nothing on the hook.

"Lost it!" he said unhappily.

Tank opened her eyes and looked at Never Ready, kneeling there at her side. Her hand went to the top of her blouse and she smiled at him. "It's all right, Anthony," she said gently.

147

"Hey!" came Frannie's call. "Are we eating fish or berries?"

Never Ready stood up and gave his hand to Tank. As though she were a lady-in-waiting at court, Tank put her hand in Never Ready's and allowed herself to be gently, ever so slowly, helped to her feet.

"Julie," Never Ready said. "Could we, maybe later . . . ?"

Tank just looked Never Ready in the eyes and smiled more dreamily than before.

As they walked over weeds and willows, Never Ready wondered if Tank knew who he was. *Maybe,* he thought, *she was dreaming I was someone else.* Maybe she wasn't even really there with him at all. He nodded to himself. He was beginning to understand why men always said they could never understand women.

Then Never Ready remembered something. Every so often, these past few days, Tank had disappeared. Not so much disappeared, really, as walked off by herself for solitude and dreaming and no one really knew what. That was where Never Ready's second chance would come. *Next time she disappears, I'm going to disappear with her.*

No one spoke much during lunch. Frannie had counted on Never Ready's failure at the pond and had gathered blackberries and wild rhubarb and clover. With what they had taken from the kitchen that morning, eating was not as unpleasant as it might have been.

Never Ready and Tank soon sank into the worries of the group. People were deep in their own minds, burrowing for memories or hopes or plans. There had been no helicopters; no pursuing motorcade. But Chanler was not forgotten. Nor was the listing read on television the night before. Though each knew himself falsely accused, falsely

148

designated "an enemy of the people," there was still an odd sense of guilt inside. Guilt and uneasiness. They could trust no one. Rely on no one but themselves. Alone and singly each wondered whether the group's strength was enough, whether they were strong enough to pick Robin from prison and get away. Whether they were strong enough to roam and raid and live on the land for however long they needed to.

Frannie jolted the group into action once again, and started toward the ridge. The day was still warm. It was only a little past two. The climb was hard, hot work.

Freddy struggled at Frannie's side, with Never Ready pushing him gently and carefully from behind. Gar and D.J. bounded and bounced along with less difficulty, but breathing heavily. Tank followed some distance behind, grasping at tree branches and roots to hoist herself up the hill, planting her feet carefully and looking ahead for footholds.

Tank had taken her arm from its sling that morning, and now found travelling was easier. She was even beginning to enjoy herself a little, beginning to feel able and strong and beginning to notice, she felt sure, that she was losing weight. After all, with irregular meals and all the running and dodging and ducking and climbing and leaping, she just had to.

Frannie called a rest midway up the ridge. Her troops gathered around her, slightly out of breath and grateful to stop. They looked for comfortable, dry, shady spots to hide in and relax enough to gather more strength for more climbing.

Neither Frannie, nor the others, noticed that Tank was no longer with them.

149

23

Beautiful Julie Wheeler swam halfway out into the pond with grace and sureness. She rolled on her back, looking down at herself, seeing the tips of her breasts break water and feeling the warmth of the sun. She rolled lazily over again and sank beneath the surface, swimming for a few seconds amid the darkness below her, seeing neither fish nor weed.

Julie Wheeler laughed when she came up for air and shook her head, feeling her hair whip back and across her face. She had never swum naked before. She loved the coolness of the water. She loved the picture of herself she imagined she saw from a distance: a beautiful, graceful water sprite diving and surfacing and singing and waving to others to join her.

Julie Wheeler was so busy being beautiful and sexy and alluring that she heard nothing but her own splashes as she swam and dove, nothing but her own laughter and song.

When she did finally hear the motor above, it was too late. She dove, screaming, and surfaced again, paddling as fast as she could toward shore. But by that time the helicopter above her made the water cold and choppy, and the net had fallen.

Chanler watched with real satisfaction as beautiful Julie Wheeler was lifted wet and nude from the pond below him, as the copter rose again with Julie Wheeler screaming in the net and terrified of struggling for fear she'd fall.

150

24

Blinded by his tears, Freddy fell against a tree as he ran, coming to his knees and crumpling into a small ball.

Gar, running behind him, scooped Freddy up in his arms and ran after the others, dodging the overhanging branches, leaping ditches, struggling down the ravine as fast as he could without dropping Freddy or falling on top of him.

Ahead of them, D.J. and Frannie were already into the shadows of the rocks that hung out over a break in the ridge. They stretched, bent and straightened, as they collected rocks they could lift and throw. They began barricading themselves into a corner, the ledges around them forming more than three sides of a square, the rock above protecting them from planes.

Gar put Freddy on his feet as he joined them and then looked back up the hill, straining to see whether Never Ready had made it. After a second he saw Never Ready's blue jacket through some shrubbery. He was coming slowly down the hillside, seeming not to hurry, seeming unaware how close danger might be.

Never Ready really didn't care how close danger was. It was he who had first noticed that Tank had fallen behind again, that she wasn't with them when Frannie called a halt. Remembering his promise to himself, at first he called for Tank softly, hoping the others wouldn't hear. Hoping that Tank was only lagging a little behind

151

some trees or rocks, looking dreamily out at the countryside, resting. He had called more loudly, though, when he
heard nothing.

Suddenly his voice had been drowned in the roar of
blades lifting upwards. Above him, above them all, Tank
had hung suspended, nude, screaming for help. The helicopter had veered east and away, taking her back, back
toward the cold and questions and perhaps even to torture.

Never Ready had stood, mesmerized, watching Tank
float noisily but gently into the distance. He couldn't believe it. She had been sitting close to him, humming,
smiling into the sun, swinging her legs through the shallow water. They had been quiet and together and touching. Touching, Never Ready remembered again, and his
eyes started to fill.

He sauntered into the makeshift camp and sank to the
ground. Freddy ran over to him for comfort. But Never
Ready sat there as though he heard nothing, saw nothing,
cared nothing. Freddy went back to Frannie's arms.

Stroking Freddy's head, Frannie took a deep breath.
"That guy who's chasing you—" she said.

"Chanler," D.J. supplied.

"Chanler," Frannie repeated. "You'd think he'd realize
if one of you were here, there would be others close by."

"Now that we have the chance, Frannie," said D.J.,
"where do we go?"

Frannie looked around. Afternoon was drawing to a
close. It would be dusk soon. They could start a fire then.
Hidden under the ledge they could feel fairly certain no
one would spot the smoke. But warmth wasn't what was
needed most. If Chanler were as close as this, they needed
a secure place, a position that couldn't be assaulted or

discovered. This place wasn't good enough.

"Raph knows the country better than anyone else," she said.

"Who cares," moaned Never Ready. "Who cares. Sooner or later they're going to win."

"Not *my* game, they're not," said Gar.

Never Ready looked into the faces of his friends. Freddy had stopped sniffling. He sat in Frannie's arms, watching Never Ready. Never Ready stared a moment back at Freddy and then motioned with one hand for Freddy to come to him. Freddy did, quickly. Never Ready felt a little stronger holding Tank's brother.

"You want to move out now or wait 'til it's dark?" Frannie asked.

"We're too close to where he got Tank," D.J. reasoned. "I think we ought to put as much distance as we can between here and wherever we're going, fast."

"So do I," Gar said.

"Let's go," Frannie replied and stood up.

They collected what remained of their belongings. Frannie and D.J. led off. Gar again carried Freddy, with Never Ready walking at his side holding Freddy's hand, ready to take the little boy if Gar got tired.

They began climbing the ridge, out of the little canyon in which they'd hidden in terror. It was suddenly a harder climb. Darkness was on its way. There was a sadness that made lifting a leg or ducking beneath trees more difficult. It took them more than an hour to reach the summit of the rise, and to look back across the plains they'd covered during the two days past.

"There's a little surprise for you all," Frannie said quietly, turning and pointing westwards.

They turned and looked down into the other valley.

153

There, in the distance, flickering jewel-like, was a huge square of light, making the whiteness of the building within whiter still and somehow smaller.

"What is it?" D.J. asked.

"That's Altoona," announced Frannie. "The prison."

Casual looks hardened into stares. There it was. After all this time.

What they saw was a circle of light, perhaps three miles away, on a plain where there were few other buildings to be seen, away from towns or crossroads. Isolated in openness. There was enough daylight remaining to see that the area was surrounded by the ridge on which they stood, and that the ridge seemed to surround nothing else. No fields or farms or even gas stations.

"Swell," Gar said. "It's impossible even to get down to it. We'd be spotted miles away."

"Don't give up so easily," Frannie advised. "Come on."

She turned northward, where the ridge began to curve around toward the distant prison. It was dark now and sudden animal sounds frightened the group, made them stop and stop breathing, staring into the blackness for what they hoped and prayed were the eyes of a squirrel or a fox.

They trudged across the ridge, staying on the highest ground. It was easier to do that though a little more dangerous, perhaps, for the natural cover on top wasn't as heavy as it was on either side. A wind began to slice through the trees atop the hill, through sweaters and jackets, through loose hair and past watering eyes.

"Frannie!" called D.J. softly. Frannie stopped.

"What?"

"Are you sure you know where you're going?"

"No," she said. "But I ain't about to stop."

154

She turned around and began again to push her way through the brush. D.J. had no choice. He followed.

For an hour more they followed Frannie, getting hungrier with each step, getting colder with each breeze that knifed past them.

"Frannie!" D.J. whispered again. "We have to stop. We can't see anything."

"Neither can she, fella."

D.J. jumped and spun around, crouched and ready to spring out in the direction of the strange voice.

"Easy, easy," the voice said. "Just hang on there. Frannie?"

Frannie had stopped at the sound of the voice. "Is that you?" she asked.

"Which you are you looking for?" the voice asked with a soft laugh.

"Raph?"

"Ah," the voice said. "You mean Raphael Ross, construction worker, prison tender, keeper of hope and hoarder of foodstuffs?"

Frannie laughed then a little, relieved. "No," she said. "I mean the one who can't see anything closer than ten feet and who gets so dizzy he always has to sit down, even if he is sitting down, before he falls down!"

"Now that one," the voice announced, "that one's right here."

25

Within a few minutes, Raph had led the group to his first cave. It was a vaulted room, almost twenty feet long and seven feet wide, hidden from the eyes of intruders or local picnickers by a passage of several feet that opened to a view of Altoona in the distance.

Along both sides of the room were boxes and tins Raph had collected on each of his circular trips. He explained that he moved from hideout to hideout, from cave to cave, night by night. Along the way he raided parked cars, broken delivery vans, and when winter came, communal kitchens on the other side of the ridge. He'd been running for nearly four years and so far, he said, pleased with himself, as far as he knew he'd never been chased or even spotted.

"But why are you hiding?" Freddy asked.

"Guess," Raph said.

Freddy looked at the man who sat on the other side of the small fire. He couldn't tell anything. The man wasn't black. He didn't seem to be handicapped. His eyes weren't slanted or his skin yellow, and he didn't speak as though he came from somewhere south, like Puerto Rico. Freddy shrugged and grinned. He couldn't guess.

Neither could D.J. He too examined Raph Ross: a tallish man who, in spite of his weathered face, couldn't have been older than thirty-five; eyes that were a cold color but held a warm look, dark straight hair that was long and hung over the collar of his workshirt and wool jacket, a nose that reminded D.J. of the Indian's nose on an ancient nickel in his coin collection.

"Wait a minute," D.J. said. "Are you an Indian?"

Raph nodded. "One of the last free ones."

"What kind?" Gar asked.

"Iroquois."

"But I thought," said Never Ready, shaking himself a little from his sadness, "that was a tribe out east somewhere."

"We were, in the old days," Raph answered. "We Iroquois and the Mohawks—part of the same tribe, really— were pretty useful for a while there. Steel workers."

"But what are you doing out here?" D.J. asked.

"That's a long story," Raph said, shaking his head. "Just say that one day, a long time ago, one day up in the rigging I got dizzy. A while later, when I couldn't hide it anymore, I got laid off."

"How long ago?" Gar asked.

"Does it matter?" wondered Raph.

"It might," Gar said seriously.

"You're a pretty tough fellow, aren't you?" Raph said. "Let's just say it was before the Government rounded up everyone—Indians and blacks and all—before I found out I'd have to run the rest of my life if I wanted to be free."

"That's what I wanted to know," Gar said, pleased.

"Some of us *did* try, you know," Raph said. "I tried, when all that happened. In my own way, I tried to show people they were wrong."

"You must have been one of the two who did," Gar said quietly.

"Maybe I was, maybe I wasn't," Raph reflected. "But

157

I went about it the wrong way. I went about it the coward's way."

"What do you mean?" asked Never Ready.

"Instead of standing straight up and shouting they were wrong, I decided I'd show them they were wrong about the Indians. I figured I'd pass for white along with the rest and then suddenly, one warm spring day when I'd done something wonderful, I would stand up tall again and announce who I was. What I was."

"What happened?" Gar asked softly.

"By the time I was ready to stand up straight, I was so ashamed of what I'd done—lied about my family and my friends, lied about who and what I was—that I couldn't stand up at all. I was trapped in my crawling. It was about then, too, that my eyes began to give out."

"You led us here," noted D.J. "There can't be too much wrong with your eyes."

"Not too much," agreed Raph, "except that I can't see anything close up. And glasses don't help. I get dizzy and have to stop and sit down to close my eyes and rest them. Remember," he went on, "I know this kind of country. I live here. I can feel my way around the whole valley."

"But how'd you get here?" Freddy wanted to know.

"Well, by the time I was beginning to get sick, I had left the east and moved slowly out here, away from the people I knew who might give me away. I just walked across the whole country and stopped here. The last job I ever worked on, as a matter of fact, was that prison you saw down there."

"You did?" Gar was astonished.

"I know that place pretty well for a blind man," Raph said.

No one spoke. "What's the matter?" Raph asked. He

158

sensed a smile running around the circle before him.

"You can help them, Raph," Frannie said.

"Help us," D.J. corrected.

Frannie smiled to herself. She wanted to be part of the group. But she hadn't been certain she was.

"Well, it sounds like you've got something pretty big on your minds," Raph guessed.

"We can talk about it in the morning," D.J. said. "I think it'd be better for us to sleep now."

Raph nodded. He stood up and felt his way toward a pile of blankets and old rainwear, outer-coats and scarves. "Take what you want," he offered. "There's plenty of warm stuff here."

Never Ready got to the pile first. He had tried to feel not so sad. He had tried to talk once in a while and to keep going, if only for Freddy's sake. But he couldn't stop feeling lonely. He couldn't stop remembering Tank's cries from the air. He couldn't stop his fingers from feeling her softness.

And he was homesick. Just a little. He felt foolish about it, but that was what he felt. He missed his father and his mother. He wondered what they were doing just then. Were they thinking about him, worrying? How he hoped so.

He pulled a blanket out and went to the farthest wall, where the warmth of the fire could still reach out and touch him. He brought the edge of the blanket up around his shoulders and turned on his heel, wrapping the woolly thing around him. He sank down and turned his face away from the fire, away from the eyes of his friends. He felt a need to cry. He hadn't been able to cry all day, ever since Tank was taken. But he couldn't hold back now, not any longer.

Freddy brought his coat and blanket over toward Never Ready. He lay down, purposely pulling up close to Never Ready so that he could reach out and touch his shoulder, so that he could pat Never Ready softly, comfortingly. Never Ready didn't turn around.

D.J. curled up and tried to force his mind to sleep. Then he threw himself over on his back and stretched out, his hands beneath his head, his eyes closed. Suddenly all he could think of was his father. What if his father really was in the same prison as Robin Frye? Would he have to rescue him, too? *Could* he? Did he want to?

Frannie found a spot for herself on the other side of the fire. Soon she had fallen into deep sleep, too tired to dream, too tired to spend a moment thinking about the day that had passed or about the day ahead. Too tired almost for anything but a smile at being finally among *other people,* accepted and happy.

Only Gar had stayed where he was, watching Raph Ross as he came back to the fire and squatted before it, holding out his hands toward the flames.

"You mind talking a while?" Gar asked him.

"No, I guess not," Raph said. "What's on your mind?"

"There are some things I don't understand, about what happened back then. Like why no one fought. Why everyone just stayed shut up and let everything happen."

"Oh boy," Raph said, shaking his head in wonder, "there are as many different reasons for that as there are people alive." He pulled a pouch of tobacco out of a coat pocket and dug his pipe into it. Tentatively he reached out toward the fire and let his fingers gently touch about for a long piece of wood that was cool enough to lift. He found one and lit his pipe.

"I'll tell you what," Raph said, letting smoke ease out

160

of his mouth, "I'll tell you how to get to sleep, instead, when you're having trouble. When you're wide awake at four in the morning and dog tired."

"But that's not what I—" Gar started to object.

"Just hang on," Raph said calmly. "Wait 'til I'm done. Then, if you want to, you can tell me you still don't understand."

Gar tried to make himself more comfortable, sitting back and patiently waiting for Raph to begin.

"Well," Raph said, settling back himself, "a lot of people have trouble getting to sleep. They toss and turn and get up to see what time it is. And nothing happens. They think about things and they get upset or angry or sad, and they just can't stop thinking and get to sleep. Some people have a theory; they'll tell you, if you want to try it, there is one sure way to get rested almost every time.

"What you do is you lie there in bed and you talk to yourself. Not loud or anything. Doesn't even have to be out loud. But you talk to yourself just the same. You start out talking to your toes. You say, 'Toes, toes, go to sleep. Toes, relax, go to sleep.' You sort of concentrate on making your toes feel sleepy and relaxed, getting the tension out of them. Then, after a minute or so, you move on up. 'Feet,' you say, 'feet, go to sleep. Relax, feet.' Pretty soon, you can feel them getting easy at the end of your bed, too.

"You move right along. 'Legs,' you tell them, 'legs, now it's your turn. Go to sleep, legs. Relax.' And then the knees, and the thighs. Pretty soon you're asleep down below, and you start on your fingers. Then your hands, and so on. You put everything at your very tips to sleep first, and then you move in on the rest of your body.

161

Most people say you'll never get far enough ever to talk to your chest, or your neck, or your head. You just concentrate like crazy on everything else and the rest just naturally falls asleep, too."

Raph smiled. "Feeling sleepy?" he asked.

"No," Gar answered seriously. "And I don't see what that has to do with our country, with what happened."

Raph nodded. "I'll try to explain it this way," he said. "Just like putting your hands and feet to sleep, those things that are farthest away from your heart—that's what happened here. Wagenson put the groups that were farthest away from the country's heart out of the way. I admit he started big. With the blacks, I mean. But that was natural because everyone was so afraid of them anyway they'd have been glad to see them disappear for any reason. But then Wagenson pulled back a bit. He went after the other, littler toes: the students, the Indians, the Japanese Americans, the Puerto Ricans. He moved along slowly, talking softly all the time. The country began to get a little sleepy, a little comfortable, as the tension in its feet and hands began to disappear. It didn't mean that the toes and fingers weren't still there. It just meant that people weren't so aware of them, or so afraid of them. And when they were put to sleep and deadened and no longer able to talk back, why Wagenson just naturally went on to the legs and the knees, to the elbows and the wrists. We got rid of the handicapped people, we got rid of the fat people. The old people got put away out of sight.

"What we had left was just the heart and mind of the country. The heart being all the regular white folks. The mind being the Government. Of course, even though that was all that was left, it was still a pretty big slice of

162

Homo sapiens. But by that time, what was left was pretty drowsy itself. What was left could hardly keep awake long enough to do anything."

"Exit and entry passes," Gar supplied. "Special Forces Units, neighborhood guards, curfews, censorship."

"Right," Raph said. "You see, it's just like being put to sleep. Just as you're drifting off, sometimes you get jerky. A leg jumps out, or an arm shakes suddenly. But by then it's too late. You're nearly there and there's nothing you can do to keep yourself awake. You just give up and drift off."

"Marching to sleep," Gar said wonderingly. "Left right, left right, hup two three four."

"There's one thing else, though, boy," Raph said. "It couldn't have happened if the people hadn't let it happen. When the Government asked them to give up something, like freedom of the press, for instance, because of an emergency or some national security problem, why, people just good-naturedly gave it up. They figured the Government must know what it was doing. If the Government said it was O.K., why, since it didn't seem to affect them any, it was O.K. by them, too."

Raph's face clouded over and he frowned. His voice became harsher, lower suddenly, as though he were finally getting angry, or as if he had been angry all the time and it was just then that he was letting his anger surface.

"And when Wagenson said, Listen, folks, you don't mind if we come in and search your homes and offices, just in case we find something illegal, 'cause there's so much illegal around—why, the people just nodded and smiled and said, Sure, if you really think it's necessary, you must know what you're doing, go ahead. As long as it doesn't seem to bother us none, why you just go right

163

ahead. And when Wagenson said he couldn't control crime and violence and the students unless he had special powers, like putting people away just because they looked suspicious or because once before maybe they'd fallen into trouble and might get into it again, why everyone nodded and said, Why not, if that's what'll get the job done?"

"But didn't *any*body, *any*where fight?" asked Gar.

Raph was silent a moment, collecting himself. "Yes," he said finally, "some people did. The students at first. And they wrote things about him in their newspapers. But pretty soon the tax people closed them down, and Wagenson himself started carting off the kids, putting them in special propaganda schools for mind-training. The regular newspapers did what they could. And the people who knew how to read, how to think about things like the Constitution and the Bill of Rights, caused a little trouble.

"But when you run up against a whole country that's tired and scared and nervous, that only wants everything to be quiet and peaceful, that only cares about whether it has enough food for a while and enough money to buy something, and that is tired, tired, tired—worse," Raph went on, getting angrier, "that is absolutely positively hungry to have somebody else do the work, do the watching and the fighting—and when somebody like Wagenson volunteers to take everything on, to handle it all and to make the country peaceful again and who has a plan for putting the troublemakers to sleep—why boy, let me tell you, those few people who wanted to fight found they weren't just fighting the President. They were fighting the whole damned country!"

Raph shook his head, trying to cool down. "One thing

more. A funny thing happened to the people who wanted to fight. They didn't want leaders but they had to have 'em. What happened was that even the nicest guy in the world, when he finds all of a sudden he's in some kind of position different, better, than his friends—even he begins to get ideas that grow bigger every minute. He's got a job. He's got responsibility. He's got power. Pretty soon even the people who most wanted to free the country found that their own leaders had gotten too far away from them to lead. Too far away from what their dreams had been. But close enough to Wagenson's dream, and susceptible, even aching to be bribed and bowed to. It was easier than anyone would ever have believed to lose this battle."

Raph took a breath. "Wow," he said. "I guess I talk too much. I hope you didn't get lost along the way."

Gar smiled. "I'm not lost."

"Anyway, that's sort of what happened," Raph said, trying to smile. "You just heard the gospel according to Saint Raphael."

Gar nodded and sat silently, thinking. He looked at the fire, flickering around the remains of the last two logs in the cave. "You know, Raph," he said, "things might change."

"I've waited, boy," Raph said. "I've waited. I begin to think now that everybody's so damned sleepy they won't ever get out of their beds and get moving."

"You're wrong," Gar told him. "My dad's out of bed. So is my mother. And us here, we're awake, out of bed. There are lots of people beginning to wake up, Raph. Not just kids, either."

"Well, I've heard little whispers here and there. I wait and wait, but the talking never gets any louder."

"It's not just the talking that counts," Gar said. "It takes time, you know."

"I know, I know," Raph said. "That's why I keep all these camps around the ridge here. No one knows about them except me. But if they're ever needed, they're perfect for hiding in and then running out, into action. If ever we get that far."

"We will," Gar said positively. "At least, I think we will."

2 6

Raph sat motionless, listening to D.J. explain why the group had come to Altoona and what they hoped to do. He nodded a little, looking neither hopeful nor worried, only thoughtful.

Never Ready sat motionless, too. He had said no more than twenty words since the night before. He felt guilty about his withdrawal, but he just didn't feel like taking part in the morning's council. He wasn't suddenly afraid. He didn't feel particularly brave. He didn't feel anything. He knew what he felt should be no different and no deeper than what Gar felt at Elizabeth's loss, or Freddy now. But he didn't care.

"Well, I'll tell you something," Raph said when D.J. finished. "If you'd tried to do this a couple years back, you'd have gotten nowhere and probably been caught in the bargain. But now I'm not so sure. They've been piling people into that place so fast, crowding them in and going out to get some more, they haven't even got enough guards to keep proper security going."

"What exactly is proper security?" Gar asked, smiling.

Raph shook his head. "You've got me there," he said. "Anyway, maybe you can do it. But you'll have to do it on your own."

"Why?" Frannie asked. "Why can't you help us?"

"I can," Raph said, "and I will. But only from here, only from the outside. I wouldn't be any use to you inside.

167

I'd probably bump into some guard who was sound asleep and send the alarms off from here to Monday."

"Are your eyes really that bad?" D.J. asked sympathetically.

"Yep," Raph said, "they really are. Oh, I can see something half a mile away. But the closer I get, the blurrier I get." He looked around. "I couldn't recognize one of you outside right now!"

"I'm Freddy," announced Freddy helpfully.

"You I'd recognize," Raph admitted. "You only come up to my waist."

"I'll grow though," Freddy assured him. "My father's nearly six feet tall."

"O.K., O.K.," laughed Raph. "Now, let's get crackin'. First off, I'll sneak into town. You can't see it from here, but on the other side of Altoona's a nice little spot where most of the people who work in the prison live. I've got one or two friends there who'll give me some food and a lot of information. Of course," he said proudly, "I already know the inside of that place like the back of my hand. I helped build it."

"Your work was probably great," Gar said, "but I don't think it's much to be proud of."

"You, boy," Raph said, "are the most unforgiving person I ever met."

Gar nodded.

"While I'm gone," Raph went on, "you all just stay put. No one ever comes around, so you're safe. That's why I've been safe all these years. Who's going to look for someone around a prison?"

"Why can't we come with you?" D.J. asked. "Or at least one of us, anyway."

"Because," Raph answered, "I assume you plan to do

168

your work at night. You'll need rest and strength and you'll have to be on your toes. Why tire yourself out ahead of time?"

"What'll we do all day?" wondered Frannie aloud.

"First off," answered Raph, "you need to know what the place looks like inside. Let's talk a bit about that before I hit the road. That way you'll have all day to plan exactly what you want to do."

"Go ahead," D.J. said.

"All right. Now, first, there aren't any wires or fences around the place. It's set in the open like it is purposely, so no one can sneak up on it or sneak away from it. But there is one time you can do both, God willing. When they turn on those lights, you can hardly see through the brightness even to look at the prison. They can't see through the light to see you looking at them from the other side of the trenches."

"What about those trenches?" D.J. urged.

"What they've got is a ring of six or seven trenches around the prison. Actually," Raph continued, "it's all one long trench that starts about eight feet out from the walls and then moves around the prison in a spiral. The trench is about two feet deep when it starts, and about eight feet deep at the outer ring."

"What's to keep us from jumping from one place to the other, from above each trench to the next spot, I mean?" Gar asked.

"Not much," Raph answered, "except the light circuits."

"What do you mean?" Frannie asked.

"Well," Raph said, "what they've got are some very strong lights somehow hooked up to a computer. The walls of the trench form a kind of V so that the lights at

169

the bottom of the trench—probably a couple hundred of them—not only give out heat and light but are reflected as well. The light forms a kind of electrical circuit. Whatever stops the light from shooting straight up and out into the night sets off an alarm. It's pretty tricky, but nothing more than we used to have in supermarkets. Electronic eyes, they were called."

"But how do the guards or whoever get in and out," D.J. wondered, "if every time they go in or out they set off the alarm?"

"They don't," Raph said. "There's no traffic in or out after dark."

"But how do *they* get across the trench?" D.J. pressed. "They must have trucks and cars with supplies."

"Mostly they use helicopters," Raph said. "There *are* two runners of plexiglas, very thick, about forty feet long. They make a track across the trenches without stopping the light from escaping upward. During the day a car or truck drives right across them and into the prison. During the night, unless the lights are off, you couldn't find them unless you knew exactly where they were."

"Do you know, Raph?" Frannie asked.

"Yes, sweetheart. I do."

Raph stood up and put on a light jacket. "Unless I get going, there won't be any raid at all," he said. He walked quickly toward the front of the cave, feeling along the walls and ceiling, his hands telling him where to turn and where to duck his head. "Rest well," he called back.

For the next few hours, Never Ready slept. Freddy puttered around and finally fell asleep sitting up, with several little pebbles before him, soldiers he had been imagining war games with. Frannie dozed off and on, and fixed lunch for whoever wanted to eat. Gar and D.J.

170

huddled together for a very long time, off by themselves, planning.

Raph returned to the cave a little before five, carrying one package under his arm and another strapped around his neck. He surrendered neither. With the five young people trailing him, Raph started down the ridge to another cave he kept ready and stocked. This hideaway put them within half a mile of the prison itself, for the ridge curved inward suddenly toward the center of the valley where the prison stood.

They made their way cautiously down the slope. Suddenly, without warning, a helicopter rose over the ridge behind them, bearing down directly at them. Frannie yelled and all six fell into leaves and bushes, furiously scavenging for whatever cover they could arrange in two seconds.

The copter whirred above them and circled the part of the ridge on which they hid. Then it flew directly at the prison, hovering a moment above the white, three-story building before sinking noisily out of sight, into the prison yard beyond the walls.

"Did you see?" Gar asked D.J. as he pulled himself up.

"Yes," D.J. said. "What do you suppose he's doing here?"

"Probably just making a wild guess," Gar said. "He still looks mean, doesn't he?"

"He always does," D.J. answered. "Chanler's always looked rotten."

Inside Raph's second cave, which was smaller than the first and better hidden, though not so well stocked or comfortable, the five sat around Raph waiting.

"O.K.," Raph said, "you guys get any bright ideas?"

171

"One," D.J. answered. "We need more time. We can't go in tonight."

"Why not?" Frannie asked.

"Because we haven't got what we need," D.J. answered. "We need something to destroy the plexiglas when we leave. We need something for the bars on Robin's window."

"That, my boy," Raph said with a broad smile, "is exactly what I've been lugging around all day. But that stuff isn't the whole story. Let's start at the beginning."

Raph pulled out his tobacco and tamped a bowl full of it. He accepted a light from Gar. "O.K., now, the building is three stories high. As far as I can tell, you only have to worry about the bottom two. You worry about the ground floor because you've got to get in. You worry about the second floor because that's where your little buddy is."

"How'd you find that out?" asked D.J.

Raph just smiled and nodded. "Never you mind. Now," he went on, "my friend in town says there's a new man helping out, a prisoner who's pretty shaky, afraid to be left alone with any of the others. He's working in the warden's records office, on the first floor. His is the second window to the left, there," Raph said, pointing out of the cave's entrance at the prison in the distance. "This guy, whoever he is, stays in that room all night. He sleeps there. He eats there. It's one of the few rooms without a Judas Walk around it."

"What's that?" asked Frannie.

"It's a secret space on three sides of a cell. People can look into a cell and watch a prisoner from certain spots in the wall."

"How do we get in?" Gar asked.

172

"That's pretty tricky. The lights go on at seven. There are a few minutes at this time of year, before the prison lights are turned on, when everything is hazy and full of shadows. You'll have to make a run for it then, across the plexiglas runners, before they turn on the circuits. Head for the window I pointed out. There's only one bar per window, stuck right in the center. The windows open from the inside. You use this super little thing," and Raph unstrung the package from around his neck.

"What's that?" D.J. asked.

"A laser," Raph answered. "Weighs a little more than ten pounds, but it's easy enough to handle. You burn through the bars if you have to. Chances are you can surprise whoever the guy in there is. After that, you're on your own. How you get to your friend and how you get him out again is what's called 'winging it.' "

"Is that all?" asked Gar, somewhat disappointed.

"Not quite," Raph said. "The prison is laid out in a square, with the exercise yard in the center of it. There's only one corridor around each floor. The prisoners eat in their rooms. The guards live in the part of the square you can't see from here, on the first floor. The kitchens are in the basement. So, incidentally, is the room where the guards change to come on and off duty."

"Where's the switch for the light circuit?" D.J. wanted to know.

"I can't help you there," Raph said. "Honestly, I don't know. It was put in after I left off working."

"All right," said D.J. "How much time do we have?"

Frannie looked at her watch. "It's just six," she announced.

D.J. nodded. "Come on, Gar," he said, walking quickly to the cave's entrance.

173

"Hey!" shouted Frannie. "What about us?"

"Not 'til we've got this figured," D.J. answered. He and Gar ducked out into the half-light outside and squatted under a tree, talking in low tones.

Never Ready, Freddy, and Frannie stood in the cave's arch and tried to hear.

"O.K.," D.J. said, as he came back into the cave. "Here's the plan," he said, kneeling down on the sandy floor. "Frannie, you and Never Ready aren't coming inside with us."

"What!" Never Ready exclaimed, alive at last.

"No," D.J. said, "we need you on the outside, to create a diversion if we need it. Frannie, you and Never Ready leave here the minute the lights come on. By that time Gar, Freddy, and I will be across the tracks and at the wall. They won't be able to see either of you through the light, so you'll be pretty safe. Never Ready, you head around to the other side of the prison, staying outside the trench. Find whatever cover you can. Take matches and paper with you, and look around for sticks or branches or dry grass. Frannie, you do the same on this side. Make two piles if you can, even three."

"That's dumb!" Frannie snorted. "What's it for?"

"If they see us and start shooting," answered Gar, "you light the fires. That'll make them think there are more of us, that there are people outside waiting to rush the place. They'll spread their gunfire then, and we'll have a chance to get out."

"Right," D.J. said. "You light the fires and then get the hell out of there. Double back here and wait for us."

"But then I won't be a part of this," Never Ready complained. "After it's all over, I won't have done anything."

174

"Besides," Frannie said, "you all wouldn't even be here if it weren't for me."

"We know that," D.J. said. "Listen, you just have to trust Gar and me. We only need three people. I mean this nicely, Frannie, but you're just a bit bigger than we can use. Do you think you could squeeze through a barred window?"

Frannie shook her head sorrowfully. "No," she admitted.

"O.K. Freddy can, if he has to. It's not that we don't want you with us," D.J. said soothingly.

"But what about me?" Never Ready asked belligerently.

"Never Ready, you're abler than Freddy is. It sounds silly, but it's true," Gar explained. "We need those fires. We need two people who can run from one fire to another faster than anyone's ever run before. We can't take a chance on Freddy's falling or stumbling."

Never Ready's face crumbled but he knew Gar was right. "Without you," Gar said quietly, "we wouldn't have gotten D.J. to join up. You're almost more a part of this than anyone else. Relax. There will be plenty of action for us all later."

"If there is a later," warned D.J.

"It's getting on," Raph interrupted. "You'd better take these, too." He handed a package to D.J. "There are two tubes of acid in there. It's for the plexiglas, in case anything happens to the laser. Use it carefully. It'll eat through pretty fast."

D.J. put the package in an inside pocket of his jacket, and draped the laser on its cord around his neck. "O.K.," he said. "You ready, Frannie?"

"Sure," she said, bending down to scoop up some paper and a few sticks that lay on the floor of the cave.

175

"Never Ready?" asked D.J.

"O.K.," Never Ready said unhappily. "I'm ready."

"I'm ready, too," announced Freddy.

"Better take this, too," Raph said. He held a knife out to Gar. Gar took it. "Thanks," he said solemnly.

"Let's go," D.J. said.

Raph stood in the cave and watched the five shadows disappear into other shadows. They wouldn't have much time. They hadn't even told him what their plan was. Perhaps they weren't certain themselves what they were going to do. He couldn't see from where he stood. He wouldn't be able to hear anything.

He turned back into the shelter of the cave, deciding there was nothing more for him to do. He wondered if the kids were strong enough to pull it off. He wondered; he doubted. But he wanted to hope, for them and for himself.

As darkness led the clock around to where the lights would be activated, Robin Frye stood at the window of his cell looking out. It had been the first day of the five since he'd arrived that he hadn't been questioned for almost six hours. He felt that something was missing, that the day had not really finished unless he was going to be faced later by accusers and investigators.

He rubbed his hand across his forehead and took his glasses off. He held the lenses up to the last rays of light outside and took out his handkerchief to clean them. He gave a start. He thought he saw something moving out beyond the trenches.

Robin snapped his glasses back onto his nose and leaned closer to the glass. He saw nothing. He shrugged. His eyes were tired. He knew without his glasses on and with tired eyes he frequently saw things he didn't see with them.

27

Frannie and Never Ready stopped at the edge of the plain where they could wait behind bushes and tall grass. They watched as D.J. and Gar ran silently across the field and onto the clear runners, into the prison grounds, ducking into the shadows of one wall.

Gar, deciding it was easier to keep his balance with Freddy in front rather than on his shoulders, carried him as an animal sometimes transports her young. Freddy hung on for dear life, bobbing in front of Gar as he ran.

"Raph was right," Gar panted, leaning against the prison wall. "That's scary."

"Seven rings," D.J. noted. "About two feet apart. How wide do you think the trench is?"

"Maybe four feet," Gar guessed. "I'd hate to have to jump it."

"What do we do now?" whispered Freddy, still clinging to Gar. Gar set him gently on the ground and pulled him back toward the wall.

"We wait, Freddy," he said. "We wait to find out if anyone saw us."

So they stood silently, lined up against the bright white wall that, within minutes, was flooded with blinding light. "What do you think they've got the trench lined with?" D.J. asked Gar under his breath.

"Who knows?" Gar shrugged. "Looks like aluminum foil, the way it shines. Probably isn't."

A few minutes passed. D.J. let his eyes rest from the glare, turning and looking up in back of him. Suddenly he threw himself to the ground and sprawled full-length against the wall.

"Down!" he commanded. Freddy and Gar responded instantly.

"What is it?" Gar asked.

"Standing up, there's a shadow. We make a shadow, heading up the wall."

They lay there tense and alert as the first dew began to gather on the grass. "D.J.," Gar grinned, "no one can see the shadows. No one's out front."

"How long do we have to wait?" Freddy asked.

As an answer, D.J. looked up the wall and pointed to the second window from the side of the prison's entrance. "Is that the one Raph meant?"

Gar nodded. "I think so."

D.J. started along the ground, crawling on his belly, using his elbows and feet to propel himself slowly over the grass. Gar and Freddy followed, Freddy simply hanging onto Gar's legs as they moved. Under the window, D.J. got to his knees and then into a crouch. Finally, he took a deep breath and stood full height alongside the window. The window was at his shoulder level. All he had to do was poke his head around for a moment to see. He stood, unmoving.

"Go ahead!" Gar urged.

D.J. looked back at Gar, obviously unwilling to start the night's action once and for all. He tried to grin. Then, carefully, he peered into the room beyond the bar and glass.

His body whipped immediately around again and flattened itself against the whitewashed concrete. His face was as white as the wall; beads of perspiration began to run down his forehead. His knees bent and he sank down to the ground.

"What's the matter?" Gar whispered.

D.J. shook his head. "We've got to get out of here," he said. "It's my old man in there."

"You mean, he's the one Raph said was new?"

"What's your father doing in there?" Freddy wanted to know.

"Shhh!" D.J. said fiercely.

Gar watched D.J.'s face a moment. "Listen," he said, "we can use him. He's not going to turn you in."

D.J. said nothing.

"Unless," Gar hesitated, "unless, well—how do you feel about him now?"

"I don't know," D.J. said miserably. "I don't know."

Gar slid up the side of the building and took a fast look inside.

"He's just finished eating," he announced when he was at ground level again. "Listen, D.J., we can't stop now. We'll have to use him. What you do afterwards is up to you, O.K.?"

D.J. just stared ahead into the light. Finally he nodded. "All right," he said. "We'll use him first, and think later."

D.J. stood up quickly, and seemed to shiver himself together. Then, without waiting, he turned around and faced the window. He knocked on it, slipping his hand through the eight-inch opening on one side of the thick vertical bar.

Inside, D.J.'s father looked up, thinking perhaps he'd imagined a sound. He saw the face at the window. He looked a second time and then a smile broke across his features. Checking the door that led into the corridor

179

first, he hurried to the window. He pulled back the glass. "D.J.!" he said happily. "You came!"

D.J. nodded solemnly. "We need help," he said. "Does this bar slide up or down?"

D.J.'s father tried the bar. "No," he said, frowning. "It's solid."

D.J. nodded. He drew the cord from around his neck and looked carefully at the laser. It didn't seem difficult.

"D.J.!" Gar whispered suddenly. "Be careful! What if it makes noise? What if its light is somehow different, or shows, or something?"

D.J. nodded. But both he and Gar knew the laser had at least to be tried. He pointed it at the bottom of the bar and pressed a lever. A thin rod of concentrated light and heat shot from an aperture in the machine and penetrated the steel bar. It took only a few seconds, and the bar was severed at its base.

Giving the steel a little time to cool, D.J.'s father grasped the bar and pulled. He was able to bend it a little near its top, but not enough.

Gar stepped up. He took the bar in both hands, near its base, and pushed with all his strength. Nothing seemed to happen but Gar turned to D.J. and smiled. Then, gathering himself together again, Gar pushed inward. The bar bent in and upward. There was enough room to crawl through.

But D.J.'s father immediately pulled a chair to the window and climbed up on it. "Wait!" D.J. commanded sharply. His father stopped in midair and looked quizzically at his son. "Not yet," D.J. said, hoisting Freddy up to the window ledge and helping him through the opening.

180

D.J. put both hands on the ledge and hoisted himself up and through the window, squeezing a shoulder in first and then pulling the rest of his body through. Gar followed and found the opening too narrow for his broad shoulders, but he twisted and squirmed and finally landed on the floor inside only a few seconds after D.J.

"We were right," Gar said. "Frannie couldn't have made it in a million years."

"Who's Frannie?" asked D.J.'s father.

"Never mind," D.J. said quickly. "Go back to where you were sitting. Do whatever you usually do, in case someone walks by."

"But—" his father started to say.

"Do it!" D.J. commanded.

His father stared at him a moment and then did as he was told. D.J., Gar and Freddy hid behind some filing cabinets.

"Now," D.J. said quietly, "we're here to get a kid named Robin Frye. Which cell is his?"

"Frye?" said his father, looking down at the papers before him. "Frye? I don't know."

"Find out," D.J. said. "You've got records somewhere. Frye. F-r-y-e," he spelled.

His father pushed his chair back and came toward the trio. He opened a cabinet drawer without looking at them and filtered through its folders. "Here it is," he announced. "Frye, Robin. Cell 22."

"Where's that?" D.J. asked.

"Almost directly above," his father answered. "About three windows to the right from here, second floor."

"Go back to your chair," D.J. directed.

"Wait!" called Gar. "Look up Bennett. Arthur Bennett."

181

D.J. nodded and understood. His father opened another drawer and began flipping through it's contents. "No," he said finally. "No one here with that name."

Gar smiled more broadly than he thought his face could stand. "Now," D.J. said, "back to your chair."

His father closed the filing cabinet and walked back. He sat down. "Now what?" he asked.

"You tell us," D.J. replied quickly. "Have you got keys to the cells?"

"No," his father said. "The only key here belongs to the Judas Walks."

"O.K.," D.J. said. "Are the corridors patrolled?"

"Not after six, when dinner's over," his father answered. "They've had to cut the guard. They've been scattered all over the country, been sent to other prisons. They've had to use them to beef up the Special Forces Units."

"How many guards are still here?" Gar asked.

"Maybe a dozen," guessed Mr. Berryman. "About one to every eight prisoners. But only half are on duty at one time, while the other half sleeps."

"When does the guard change?" D.J. asked.

"Every four hours. They changed a couple hours ago, at six."

"O.K.," D.J. said, turning to Gar. "That leaves us almost two hours."

Freddy looked up at D.J. "Are we going to bring your father with us?" he asked.

D.J. didn't answer. "D.J.," said his father, "are you?"

"Where are the guards?" D.J. dodged.

His father sighed. "There are two at the gate. One atop each corner. There are some visitors here, too, but they're in the basement quarters. Chanler, D.J."

"I know," said D.J.

182

"D.J.?" asked his father again.

D.J. said nothing for a long moment. "We'll see," he said.

"I'm your father," Mr. Berryman reminded him.

"Swell," said D.J. bitterly. "Go to the door," he commanded. "Look out. Tell us what you see."

They heard Mr. Berryman's chair scrape on the cement floor as he stood. They waited. "Nothing," he announced. "It's clear."

D.J. stood. Then Gar, and Freddy, who smiled pleasantly at Mr. Berryman as he came out from behind the cabinets.

"Let's go," D.J. said.

"Where?" his father asked.

Gar drew the knife Raph had given him. "Upstairs," he said.

Mr. Berryman looked at the blade. "You don't need that," he said.

Gar did not answer.

"Bring the key to the Walks," D.J. commanded.

His father opened a cabinet and took a key from a hook. He handed it to D.J.

They were in the corridor. It, too, was white and well lit. There was no one ahead of them and no one behind. They walked slowly and silently along a wall toward a stairway.

Before starting up the steps, D.J. stopped and took the key he held and tried the lock on the last door near the stairs. The door swung outward without a sound. Telling Gar to wait, D.J. entered the Judas Walk, leaving the door partly open behind him. Ahead, at eye level, was an opening, covered with tinted, grainy-looking glass. D.J. guessed that a prisoner in a cell could not tell that an opening had been made since the grainy covering matched the wall inside the cell.

The cell wasn't large, perhaps eight by six feet. A man inside lay on his bed, his legs stretched out and braced on top of a rolled-up blanket so that they bent at the knees and kept the soles of his feet off the other blanket beneath. The man's eyes were closed to the bare bulb above, and his right arm was bent over his face. D.J. could not see what the man looked like but he could see, by moving around a corner to a second glass opening, the soles of his feet. They had been beaten. They were swollen and scarred and black with bruises. D.J. felt sick. He turned quickly away and stepped back into the hall, closing the Judas Walk's door behind him.

He looked at his father. D.J. no longer had any doubt. He knew what he wanted to do with him. If his father were even partly responsible for things like what he had just seen, D.J. knew he deserved treatment of the same kind.

Mr. Berryman could not yet read his sentence in D.J.'s eyes. But what he saw made him uneasy—a combination of hate and fear and sorrow and determination. He bowed his head to avoid D.J.'s eyes.

"Let's go," D.J. said softly, finding it difficult to speak at all.

Slowly, stopping to listen for alien sounds, D.J. led the three up the stairs. Freddy held tight to Gar's hand. Gar's other hand held the dagger, pointing toward Mr. Berryman's back.

At the top of the stairs, D.J. stopped. "Which way?" he asked.

His father nodded to the right.

"This is too easy, D.J.," Gar whispered. "I don't believe it."

D.J. nodded. The same thought had come to him.

Easing into the hallway, the four began sliding along the smooth walls. They stopped every few steps to listen. They heard nothing. They waited and started again. Gar kept shaking his head in disbelief.

Outside Cell 22, they stopped. D.J. slowly turned the key in the lock and pulled the Judas door outward. Gar and Freddy peered into the hdarkness. They could just make out a series of five locks on the steel cell door. "Jesus!" Gar gasped. "What happens if there's a fire?"

D.J. motioned them all to enter the Judas Walk. When they were inside the narrow corridor lining three sides of Robin's cell, he closed the door behind them. He took a deep breath and sighed. They would be safe now, for a while at least.

They stood single file, close to one another against one wall. "Listen," said D.J., "from what I saw downstairs, Robin may not be able to walk. He may be pretty badly battered. Freddy, he's your friend. Try not to be upset by how he looks, O.K.?"

Freddy nodded. "O.K.," he said. "I won't say anything, I promise."

"Good," D.J. said. He and Gar together stepped to the glass opening and looked into the cell.

Robin was seated on his bed. He wore his shoes and socks. D.J. sighed with relief. "He's O.K.," he turned to tell Freddy.

"Let's go around the other side," Gar said. He led the three around a corner and he and D.J. looked again through an opening of treated glass.

185

Robin, on his bunk, was writing something in a small notebook. He was concentrating. He could neither hear nor see his visitors. His curly red head bobbed from time to time as he wrote, and once he looked up and seemed to be staring directly at Gar and D.J.

Gar lifted Freddy to the window. "But what's he wearing?" Freddy asked. "Those funny clothes?"

Gar set Freddy down. "It's the prison uniform, I think," he said.

"Now what are you going to do?" Mr. Berryman asked.

"I'm not sure," D.J. said. "What do you think, Gar?"

"Well, it would probably take less time to use the laser on the glass here then to try to get all five locks," Gar reasoned.

"O.K.," D.J. said, thinking this over. "We'll break it," D.J. smiled, "and probably scare the daylights out of Frye doing it."

"Well," Gar reflected, "why not hold Freddy up, ready, so that when it breaks, his face will be the first one the kid sees?"

"All right," D.J. agreed. "But we've got something else to do first." He loosened his belt.

"What?" asked Gar.

"This!" D.J. said suddenly, whirling around and grabbing his father's hands. Swiftly he looped his belt around them, binding them together in a useless knot.

"D.J.!" said his father. "What is this? Why are you—?"

"Shut up!" commanded D.J. under his breath. "Just shut your goddamned mouth!"

Holding his father's wrists in one hand, he reached into a back pocket with his other and drew out a handkerchief. "Turn around," he ordered.

Mr. Berryman looked sadly at his son. "Do I really de-

186

serve this, D.J.?" he said. "Do you really hate me so?"

"I said shut up!" D.J. answered, pushing his father around. "Gar, get his legs."

Gar bent down with his own belt in hand and bound Mr. Berryman's ankles. D.J. wrapped his handkerchief around his father's jaws, gagging him. Then, roughly, using his own knees to bend his father's, he pushed him quickly and brutally to the floor of the Walk.

"O.K. We can get started now," D.J. said. He handed the laser to Gar.

Gar took the machine and aimed it at the ledge where the glass window was imbedded in concrete. He pushed the lever.

The light narrowed in on the window pane, and the burning made a slight hissing sound as Gar directed the laser along the glass.

Inside, Robin looked up at the tiny soft sounds. In five days, it was the first foreign sound he'd heard. He put his notebook down. There seemed to be a glimmering line across the wall, higher than he was tall.

Gar directed the beam back and across the window ledge again. Then he set the laser down on the floor of the Judas Walk. "Ready?" he asked D.J.

D.J. nodded, and picked up Freddy.

Wrapping both hands in his jacket, Gar doubled up his fists and, grinning for no reason, slammed them into the glass where it had been burned. The window gave way.

"Robin!" Freddy nearly shouted. "Robin, it's me, Freddy!"

Robin stood in his cell, staring at the face that seemed to float on the wall. Then he rushed across to the hole. "Freddy!" he said. "What are you doing here?"

"We're here to rescue you!" Freddy announced proudly, beaming down at his friend. "We're going to rescue you!"

Robin stood looking up. Suddenly Freddy's face disappeared and it was D.J.'s face at the opening. "Don't be frightened," D.J. said quickly. "Please, don't be nervous."

Robin's smile instantly faded. He stood silently, waiting.

"It will take us a while longer," D.J. said. "But we'll get in. Just stand back, O.K.?"

Robin moved a few steps back and waited, still somber.

In the Judas Walk, Gar took his knife and began scraping at the cement below the broken window. The window itself was barely twelve inches high. Freddy might be able to get through the opening now, but he knew he and D.J. never would. He chipped away at the porous concrete. Bits and pieces flew into the cell and into the walkway.

"What's the time?" he asked D.J. urgently.

"Just nine," D.J. said.

"Haven't you got anything sharp?" Gar asked.

D.J. searched his pockets. All he found was a little change and his car keys. He shrugged and brought the keys out and began chiseling, too.

D.J.'s father, on the floor, watched the boys work for a while, and then he closed his eyes. He wasn't afraid. He even admired his son a little. D.J. was, after all, being no more ruthless than he himself had been every day for many years. In a way, he even felt a little proud.

By nine-fifteen, Freddy was standing in Robin's cell, glowing. "You look funny," he said to his friend.

"So do you," Robin answered. "Where have you been? Your clothes are ruined."

"All over," Freddy announced happily. "We've been all over, hiking and climbing and running."

188

D.J. eased himself through the opening and jumped down into the cell.

Robin faced him solemnly. Without thinking, one hand went to his glasses as though he feared D.J. would again take them from his nose and smash them into the floor.

"Relax, kid," D.J. urged. "We're here to help."

Robin did not look convinced, but Freddy's enthusiasm and Freddy's smile made him feel a little better.

"Why is Freddy here?" Robin asked D.J.

D.J. was at a loss for a moment. Then he remembered. "Because he was in danger. Someone found out about his foot."

That made sense to Robin. He wondered who had found out. He nodded at D.J. "O.K.," he said, convinced.

"There's an Indian outside," Freddy announced. "And we've got a black girl, too!"

Robin smiled at Freddy's smile. "On our side?"

Gar eased into the room. There was a small stream of blood coming from one of his shoulders where the glass of the window had not all fallen free and where he had scraped himself trying to squeeze through. He dabbed briefly at it and then walked to Robin's window. Motioning for silence, he drew back the thick glass until only the bar separated them from the night air beyond.

Everyone stood still, listening. They could hear nothing that indicated danger. Through the window, all they could see was the incredible light shimmering up into the darkness, cutting the prison off from the world beyond the trenches.

Gar turned back into the room. "How are you feeling?" he asked Robin.

"All right," Robin answered. "Tired. They never turn our lights off."

189

"But you're O.K. otherwise?" Gar wanted to know.

Robin nodded.

"O.K.," Gar said. "I guess now we just sit tight a while."

"Why?" Robin asked. "What happens next?"

"We're not sure," D.J. answered him. "We know the guards change in less than an hour. That's probably the best time."

"For what?" asked Robin severely. "It could be the worst time. I mean, if they're moving around already, it's easier for them to get into action. If half of them are off duty, sitting down or maybe even sleeping, they'll need more time to get moving," he advised.

D.J. looked at Robin. Then he grinned. "Pretty smart, for a kid."

Robin stiffened. "If you know better, do what you want," he said coolly.

"No," D.J. said quickly. "I think you're right, I really do." He turned to Gar. "Don't you?"

Gar nodded. "We'd better start, I guess," he said.

"O.K.," said D.J., motioning Freddy and Robin over to the cell window. "Here's the way it works. Gar, you take out the bar, like downstairs." Gar nodded. "Then, gang, we jump."

D.J. looked out the window. "It's not so bad as it looks," he said reassuringly. "Gar can go first, and then. . . ."

Gar laughed. "Thanks, buddy!"

"Well," D.J. said, "O.K., then I'll go first. Then Robin, you jump. I'll try to break your fall. Freddy's next. Gar, you come last."

Everyone nodded agreement.

"The minute we're all safe on the ground," D.J. continued, "we sneak along the wall, toward the gates. Then, together, we can make a run for it. Gar," he went on," I

190

think we'll have to carry Freddy then."

"You take the acid, you and Robin, just in case," said Gar. "I'll bring Freddy."

"No," D.J. said, frowning. "That's the trouble. You and Freddy have to start out ahead of us. Otherwise, if we have to use the acid, it will be working as you try to get across. We don't know how fast it would eat through."

"Let's stop talking and get going," Gar said impatiently. He pushed D.J. away from the window and tried at first to loosen the single bar without the laser. Nothing moved. He took the portable machine and aimed it at the bottom of the bar. The lever was pushed and within seconds the bar was broken. Gar pushed and the bar swung outward. He pushed some more and bent it upward, out into the light.

"Ready?" Gar asked as he stepped back.

D.J. grinned. "I guess," he said, hoisting himself onto the ledge. He looked down. Ten feet, maybe twelve, wasn't much. But it looked like a mile suddenly. He swung around on his perch and hooked his hands over the ledge inside the cell. He let himself ease carefully out the window, legs first. He held himself suspended a minute, and then disappeared.

Gar looked out the window. D.J. was getting up. He moved quickly to the wall and signalled he was all right. Gar turned around and helped Robin Frye onto the ledge. Holding Robin's hands, Gar leaned out and dropped him gently into the air. D.J. managed to catch him and together they fell silently onto the grass.

No one moved. There were no sounds. The guards were still unaware of their presence.

"Freddy," Gar said, lifting him up to the window, "it's your turn."

191

"I'm ready," Freddy grinned. He looked down and saw Robin and D.J. hovering against the wall." "Here I come!" he whispered, as Gar took his hands and let him fall the few feet into D.J.'s arms.

As he fell through the air, Freddy giggled.

He and D.J. fell together toward the wall. A moment of stillness was broken by a cough. One of the guards on a tower—they couldn't be certain which tower—had coughed. But there was no alarm.

Gar hopped onto the ledge, laser in hand, and jumped straight out, in a hurry now, nervous and anxious to do the rest and to get away. He sailed through the air and landed on his side, groping for the laser. He had leapt with too much speed, too much eagerness. The machine fell out of his grasp and into the trench.

Without thinking, Gar tried to reach down into the trench to retrieve the laser. He couldn't reach it. The heat from the beams at the trench's base seemed to scorch his hand.

The siren began slowly, as though it was unused to making any sound at all and needed to clear its throat first.

Gar jumped to his feet and ran to the wall. "Get going!" he said hoarsely. "Let's get out of here!"

He grabbed Freddy and slung him onto his back as Robin and D.J. ran toward the gates of the prison, the gates that could swing open at any moment.

By the time all four had reached the edge of the plexiglas, the siren was in full cry, sending its terrifying sound out across the valley. So far no guard had shot, no guard had appeared in the gateway, no spotlights had begun circling.

D.J. crouched, opening the two vials. He handed one to Robin. "Trail this behind you," he commanded. "Make it last as long as you can." He held the other container. He doubted the acid would last the forty feet across the runway and out into the night, but they could do enough damage with it to keep a truck or armored car from sailing out to chase and hunt them down.

He looked quickly at each fugitive. He sensed they were ready. With Freddy aboard, bobbing on his shoulders and sliding from side to side, Gar went first, running as fast as he could, running nearly out of control to where the plexiglas began to lead away from the prison.

Robin and D.J. followed, running more carefully in order not to spill anything from the open vials.

As they hit the thick plastic, D.J. and Robin crouched as they ran, each with an arm trailing behind, the acid spilling out and starting instantly to eat the plexiglas.

D.J. stopped a moment to examine the damage. The acid didn't seem to be eating all the way through. He wanted to reach down and touch the spot where it stopped, to see how hot it was, to guess whether in fact it would do what he hoped. But he dared not. He half-stood again and began to run. He ran into and nearly fell over Gar and Freddy, crumpled a few feet ahead of him.

"Keep going!" Gar hissed at him. "We'll be up in a second. It's damned slippery!"

D.J. started to reach out for Freddy but Gar held him tight. "Don't stop!" Gar shouted above the sirens. "We'll make it. Get the hell out of here!"

D.J. didn't know what to do. The noise and the heat and the light and Gar's commands confused him. He pulled up and started to back away, along the plexiglas path. He turned finally and, remembering, let the acid trail out behind him on the slick surface as again he moved toward freedom.

Gar struggled to his feet and hoisted Freddy to his back. Then he stood, swaying a moment, fearful for the first time of falling over into the trench. He took one step and then another, testing his balance, and then he began to speed up.

He could hear the gates finally opening behind him. Because of the light from the circuits that surrounded him, Gar couldn't tell whether trucks or cars had headlights on. He *could* hear, though, motors revving and beginning to move out toward him.

He began to run again and then stopped almost immediately. "What's the matter?" Freddy shouted. "Gar, what's the matter?"

"The acid!" he shouted. "It's eaten the track away!"

Wildly, Gar looked about. He stood on the plastic in between two trenches. He could feel the heat beneath his shoes, the acid eating the plastic down to the grass. He couldn't see; the lights were blinding. He lowered himself to his knees and began crawling off the plexiglas onto the grass that ran between the trenches. The heat of the plastic and the remaining acid burned into his palms and through his trousers.

Freddy hung on for dear life. Suddenly he felt grass. Gar had sprawled full-length on the ground.

"Hang on, Freddy!" Gar shouted. "We're going to try to jump it!"

Gar crawled a few more yards off the track, feeling almost certain that the guards wouldn't be able to see him between the rays of powerful light that shot upward. When he was perhaps fifteen feet into the circle, he rose to his knees and then, more carefully, he stood. Freddy had become so heavy; Gar swayed as he stood trying to squint through the beams to see how far he had to jump.

"Ready?" he shouted to Freddy.

"O.K.!" Freddy shouted back, tightening his grip around Gar's neck.

Gar pulled his muscles tight. He took a breath. There was not enough space where he stood to move back and try to run forward, to get up speed. He had to guess blindly. He guessed. He leapt.

"Eeee!" Freddy screamed as they hit the ground.

Gar struggled to stay on the grass, not to fall into the beams below. They were safe.

Behind him, machine guns opened fire, shooting wildly into the light, sweeping the circle searching for a body to rip in half.

"Jesus!" Gar said aloud. "We'll just have to keep going, Freddy!" he shouted. "Pray!"

As he stood and gathered his strength, he heard the roar of huge motors on his left: the trucks had started across. Gar held his breath and jumped another trench.

Freddy didn't scream. He held on with his eyes shut, and prayed.

Again they hit solid ground.

Just then there was an explosion. The sound wave hit first, and then a wave of shock and heat. Gar, already down with Freddy on his back, put out his hands to steady himself. He tried to look to his left, but the sudden extra fierce heat made him turn back immediately.

He realized what had happened. The car that had started out first in pursuit had hit the plexiglas, which had given way, or perhaps hadn't even been there where the driver had expected it. Gar guessed that a second car or truck had probably pushed the hood of the first into the heat and the light of the circuits, and gasoline had ignited.

195

As he stood, he tried to reach around to pat Freddy's back. "Only one more," he said consolingly. "I think there's only one more, Freddy!"

"O.K.," Freddy shouted. "I'm ready!"

Gar stood a moment, praying for the strength to make this last leap into space. He could hear the machine guns coming closer and closer, and suddenly, before him, he saw gasoline spreading in the trench. The flames that followed it weren't more than ten feet away. He'd have to jump now or be caught between the two fires.

He jumped. In midair he felt Freddy shift suddenly, almost losing his grip around his neck. And then he felt something hit his shoulder.

He and Freddy landed. In darkness. Safely across. Gar smiled as he rolled over. There *was* something wrong with his shoulder but he wasn't certain what and he didn't, at that moment, care.

D.J. and Robin were at his side in an instant. He looked up at them gratefully as they tried to get him and Freddy to stand. Out of the corner of his eye he saw one of the fires that Frannie or Never Ready had lit. He felt weak.

Freddy still clung to his back, silently.

"Gar!" D.J. shouted. "Can you run?"

"I guess so." Gar's voice sounded very far away to him. "Point me somewhere."

He struggled to stand, Freddy still aboard. D.J. pointed to a distant, wavering light. "Raph's got a light on. Can you see it?"

Gar squinted. "Yes," he said at last. Haltingly, he started forward. D.J. ran alongside him, one hand on Freddy to steady him.

Behind them, as they neared Raph's cave, they heard

the roar of a helicopter. Robin looked back and saw a black shadow rising out of the flames, its rotors fanning the gasoline fire below. "Hurry!" he shouted. "Hurry!"

Frannie and Never Ready stood aside as the four burst into the cave. Raph turned off his torch and tried to secure the cave's entrance. A lantern glowed faintly at the rear.

Gar entered and fell forward, unconscious. Freddy fell with him, never uttering a word of surprise.

The helicopter rose from the prison and, its searchlights flashing, began circling the trenches. Finally, someone inside the prison switched the circuits off. Frannie saw the scene suddenly change as night retook its rightful place, as the orange flames of the gas fire slithered up into the air and fell exhausted back again into the trench. The helicopter stayed out of range of the fire, looking like a frantic old woman caught by fear and rushing from room to room, not knowing where to hide.

28

Freddy could hardly keep his eyes open. He looked up into the anxious faces above him and smiled. Then his breathing stopped.

Frannie started to cry softly, her sobs shaking her whole body.

Never Ready turned away. Elizabeth and Tank and now Freddy. He was angry. He was more than that—furious, disgusted, heartsick. He wanted to do something, but he wasn't certain what. If only he had gone to the prison instead of Freddy.

D.J. stood up and walked slowly back to the rear of the cave where Gar lay, shivering with fever chills. The bleeding had finally stopped, but Raph said he thought that Gar would never be able to use his right arm again. It would hang useless from his shattered shoulder, pushed this way and that by the winds of life.

"Freddy's dead," D.J. said, hunching down near Gar.

Gar nodded weakly. "We've got to get out of here," he said.

"We can't," Robin said quietly, wiping his eyes with a sleeve and then putting his glasses back on his nose. "Frannie says they're all over the valley. It's better to sit here and wait a while."

"Besides," said Raph, "where can you go?"

"To get Elizabeth," Gar said faintly. "I made a promise. Find my parents."

"All right," D.J. said. "We will. We'll try to get Elizabeth out."

"No!" said Gar sharply. "You don't *try!* You *do* it!"

"Then what?" asked Raph.

"Well," D.J. said, leaning against a wall, "I guess then we try to join forces with other people. Try to tie up with Gar's folks."

"Are there others? Really?" Raph asked.

"Yes," Robin answered instantly. "That's all I ever heard, in prison. That's all they ever asked me about. Who else was in the Underground, who else did I know, how did I get into it, who recruited me, who were the leaders."

"That's good," Gar nodded. "That's really good. People are awake at last."

"We'll come back for you, Gar," D.J. said. "As soon as we can, we'll come back for you."

"I won't be much use, I guess," Gar said.

"Yes, you will," D.J. tried to reassure him. "We'll bring a doctor with us."

"Hey!" Frannie called softly to them.

D.J. stood up and went to the entrance of the cave. Frannie was lying on her stomach, peering out through the leaves and branches that camouflaged the cave from outside view. Her face was still wet with tears, but her eyes were busy scanning the valley. "I think they've stopped," she said. "They seem to be regrouping, outside the trench. See?"

They watched as a group of uniformed guards, standing nervously around the smoking trench, began to line up single file. Then, one after another, they stepped back a few paces to get a running start, leaping one trench and then a second and then a third until finally they disappeared through the prison gates.

"Do you think Chanler was in one of those cars?" Frannie asked D.J.

"Who knows? Maybe he was safe in the helicopter. I guess only time will tell," D.J. said dully. "If he's alive, he'll know who got Robin out."

As he and Frannie watched, three helicopters soared over their heads and headed toward the prison, hovering and then dropping behind its walls.

"Never Ready!" D.J. called suddenly. "Robin!"

The two moved quickly to his side. "I think we'd better hit the road," D.J. announced.

"So do I," Frannie agreed. "It's better for us to start out when they're all inside the prison, deciding what to do. At least we can cover the first few miles without watching for planes and hiding every few steps."

"What about Freddy?" Robin asked. "We can't just leave him."

"I'll take care of him," Raph said, standing close to the quiet body. "When everything's calmed down a bit in the morning, I'll take him up the hill a ways and bury him. Face up," he added, "and smiling."

Robin nodded and turned away, pretending to adjust his glasses.

"We've got to get Tank, too," Never Ready said. "Do you suppose they'll still be in the same place, Tank and Elizabeth?"

"I hope so," D.J. answered. "We'll just have to hurry."

Frannie turned around to crawl to Freddy's side. She reached out for his hand and held it a moment in her own, turning it over and then turning it back again, remembering.

200

After another moment, she stood and smiled warmly at Gar. "See you," she said.

Gar smiled back as best he could. "Good luck, Frannie," he said.

Frannie nodded.

"Raph," D.J. said, "if you get into town again, tell your friends about us, will you? Maybe they can spread the word ahead of us. Maybe it won't be so hard that way, finding others who are fighting. Maybe they'll even find us instead. We're going to be a little tired."

Raph nodded. "I wish I knew some of my own language," he said. D.J. and Frannie and Never Ready and Robin stood at the cave's entrance, ready to leave. "Indian words for 'Love' or 'Soon' or maybe 'Peace'."

"Peace," D.J. said, smiling. He took Raph's hand.

"Soon," added Never Ready.

"And maybe," Robin said, "just maybe, it'll be Peace Now."

"And love forever," Frannie said, as she ducked through the underbrush. The others followed her.

Raph felt their footfalls above his head and wished he had been able to see them, to see them really clearly, just once before it was too late.